The Escape
to
Candyland

Share Your Thoughts

Want to help make *The Escape to Candyland* a bestselling novel? Consider leaving an honest review of this advance reader copy on Goodreads, on your personal author website or blog, and anywhere else readers go for recommendations. It's our priority at SFK Press to publish books for readers to enjoy, and our authors appreciate and value your feedback.

OUR SOUTHERN FRIED GUARANTEE

If you wouldn't enthusiastically recommend one of our books with a 4- or 5-star rating to a friend, then the next story is on us. We believe that much in the stories we're telling. Simply email us at pr@sfkmultimedia.com.

SFK
PRESS

The Escape to Candyland

Yong Takahashi

For my husband

and

All my fellow writers—

Be brave. Keep writing.

CONTENTS

American Dreams

I've been married to Joanna Richards for three years, eleven months, and twenty-eight days. This may sound like we're getting ready to celebrate our fourth anniversary. For my co-workers, they know better. It's a sham.

My former boss, Lisa Liu, arranged the marriage. She brought me to Georgia from Shanghai eight years ago. In exchange for working in her kitchen, she promised to provide a place for me to sleep in her basement, a small wage, and a Green Card.

Every month, I send money to my girlfriend. I gave her an American name, Betty. It sounds like it goes with my American name, Benny. I wanted her to get used to it before she came here. Even after I divorce Joanna, it may be years before Betty can move to America. I hope our son gives her comfort until then.

Betty says she understands my situation, but what woman would believe that nothing is going on between Joanna and me? I reassure her that Joanna didn't marry me out of the goodness of her heart. Lisa gave her five thousand dollars. She was one of the first customers of the restaurant and has had a crush on Andy, the owner's son, ever since.

I met Lisa through my cousin. He and Lisa's ex-husband used to play poker together. Lisa asked my cousin to find a cook for her since her husband went missing most of the time.

Somebody's angry wife broke up the big card game down in Jonesboro about six months ago. Johnny lost a huge hand; I heard it was over sixty thousand dollars. He had taken Lisa's Lottery Club money to gamble with. Then he ran away, leaving her to bear the mantle of shame.

The Lottery Club was a fund that several chosen and

trusted members of the Chinese community contributed to each month. The amount and length of time was agreed upon by the group. Since Lisa's business was doing well, she was chosen to hold the money. Each member contributed five thousand dollars per month. Every month, one member received fifty thousand dollars to improve their business. The goal of this exercise was to let each member have a large sum for things such as expansion or purchasing real estate. At the end of ten months, and after every member received their payout, they decided if they would participate again.

When her husband stole the funds, Lisa had to come up with the money to cover the monthly payment. Worse, she lost face. In our community, pride is the most valued commodity; it's worth more than money, more than a spouse, more than a son.

Lisa's friend, Jenny Tanaka, agreed to cover the stolen money and pay an extra fifty-thousand dollars to buy Lisa's restaurant. Lisa had brought her into the Lottery Club even though Jenny was Japanese. The other members balked, but Lisa forced them into it. Lisa and Jenny hoped their two socially awkward children would marry one day and grow their restaurant empire in the northern suburbs.

Lisa had been considering expanding to Milton, which used to be part of Alpharetta. Lisa said the tennis-playing housewives there act civilized, not like the screaming lunatics down here, only forty minutes away.

Grace, the new part-time waitress, tells us the rich people are moving to the new cities in north Fulton County. She attends Georgia State University. Her parents own a small dry cleaners in Marietta, a city they chose for its good schools. As a compliant Chinese daughter, Grace will become a doctor. She really wants to run a food truck, but for ethnic parents, running a food truck is not an acceptable goal.

"Sweating, scrimping, and hustling are for non-educated people," they tell her.

Hearing about Milton makes Andy more nervous than usual. He normally flutters around the front of the restaurant and interacts with the customers. But lately, he's quiet, sitting behind the counter playing Candy Crush on his iPhone.

Joanna tells me Andy wants to be a painter. "He's gifted," she boasts. She has one of his paintings in her room. It's pretty good. Not museum good, but with training, she supposes he might be able to make a living doing it.

"He's applied to Savannah College of Art and Design," she continues. He has saved his tips since he was a boy. Lisa surely couldn't pay for his tuition now, even if she wanted to.

The last time Jenny was here, she asked the staff if they knew other people who want to work here. She plans to live with her doctor daughter in Buckhead and help raise her grandchildren while Andy and her younger daughter, Kaze, run the restaurants.

She has to be careful, ICE is really cracking down on illegals. The police could storm the restaurant at any time. We saw a line-up near the farmer's market last weekend. The Hispanics were standing in a line, strung together with zip-tie handcuffs. We drove past them, most of us lying down in the back of the van.

If Grace gets the nerve to start a food truck business, I want to go with her. But I know unless Jenny gets a percentage of my profits, she won't let me go. I owe her too much as my debt to Lisa was transferred to her. My mother needed an operation last year and Lisa paid for that, too. I feel like I'm drowning.

Joanna says she has enough money saved up from living at Lisa's house to buy her own place. She needs to clear up some old debts and then the bank will loan her the rest of the money. I will have to go with her. If the U.S. Citizenship and Immigration Service does a home inspection, we must look like we live together. Although we don't really sleep together, clothes and personal effects need to be strewn together. Photos of our intertwined lives have to be placed carefully around our house.

"We should stay married past the minimum wait period so we don't raise suspicion," says Joanna. She is tall, even for an American woman. She towers over me. I step back.

"Betty won't wait much longer," I explain to her. "What about my son? He's getting older. Soon, he won't know who I am."

"We can bring him over here. I can adopt him."

"Betty won't allow such foolishness," I say.

"I think she will," says Joanna.

"How will I explain the situation to my son?"

"Tell him we're roommates, or we were married before. I'm your ex. Immigration will come for one final interview, then we can rearrange the house. Take down our photos."

She makes things sound so simple. She's a simple woman with simple thoughts, happy working as a security guard at a halfway house. She tells me stories of how these women screwed up their lives. After a brief stay at the house, they are given their own apartments by a charity. The government helps them get back on their feet.

What a beautiful country. I hope they appreciate it.

Lisa's house is currently on the market. We may all be on the street very shortly. Andy has arranged to move in with Joanna if he's accepted into his art program. Joanna is happy to let him stay with her. She's convinced she'll marry Andy when we divorce. But I don't think he'll ever move in with her—or go to SCAD. The boy has had other dreams before—fashion designer, interior decorator, even becoming a chef. Lisa tells him it wouldn't make sense to go to cooking school when he could learn from us. Lisa explained Americans like what they like—almond chicken (chicken tenders with gravy), sweet and sour chicken (chicken nuggets with pineapple sauce), teriyaki wings (drenched in sticky sauce), and fried rice (soaked in soy sauce).

She has never let him try anything new. If it's not her idea, it's not a good one. She has shot down Andy's ideas of beef satay, lettuce wraps, shrimp egg rolls, and orange-roasted chicken.

Andy pretends the new restaurant is not happening but in six months, it will be ready. He'll be chained to a new place, unable to escape.

Grace says it will cost over one hundred thousand dollars to start the food truck. I wonder where I'll get even a small amount of that money. After Jenny inspects the kitchen and leaves, Grace and I plan our menus. She says everyone is doing fusion, now. Our working name is Chi-Mex, which stands for Chinese and Mexican.

She says there is a food truck park off Howell Mill Road in Atlanta. If we can't get in there, we can go to the smaller, non-permanent locations. The smaller cities like Kennesaw and Marietta are hosting food truck days. We'd have to travel around, but that will be the hardest part.

"Nothing is as hard as living in China," I inform her.

"I've had that drilled into my head," she says. There's plenty of guilt there, and she doesn't have room for any of my sad stories. Her father was an engineer and her mother was a teacher in China. They gave up their status and moved here for their children.

"Sorry." I put my hands in my pockets and look away from her. It feels strange apologizing to a girl who could technically be my daughter. Such conversations between generations doesn't happen often in our community. I know, I'm in America now. So I have to adapt.

"It's cool," she says. She flips her hair.

"We can apply for an SBA loan," she tells me.

"What is this?" I ask.

"Small Business Administration. Here, I downloaded it. They loan money to small businesses." She pulls out a folder. "I used the food truck scenario as a project for marketing class. I got an A."

"Congratulations," I say.

"Everyone in class, including the professor, said it's a good idea."

"I can't leave this place. I owe Lisa—I mean Jenny—so much money."

"She pays you under the table. What she's doing is illegal. She's not going to risk getting into trouble."

"I can't walk out on my debt. It's not right."

"What if we cut her in on it?" she asks.

"Cut?" I ask.

"Include her as a partner. She's a witch, but she's a good business woman. She can't deny it's going to work."

"You've thought a lot about this," I say.

"I don't want to be a doctor. With all the malpractice insurance I'd have to pay, how much would I really be making?"

Grace suggests I ask my cousin for my portion of the money.

"No, his wife wouldn't allow it," I tell her. She won't let him send money to his own family. That would cut into her betting money. I'd rather ask Joanna, even though she and Grace don't get along.

Jenny arrives in the Mercedes her daughter bought for her. She shows the Milton floor plans to Andy.

"Why are you going so far north? They don't like people like us up there."

"Who cares? When we came here twenty years ago, we weren't welcome on Buford Highway. Times change."

"I'm thinking about going to school," says Andy.

"You're twenty-eight years old. It's too late for school. You see these kids go to college and can't find jobs. Mr. Park, the man who owns the gas station on the corner, is so upset. His son went to Emory, spent one hundred twenty thousand dollars in tuition, and can't find a job. The son is working behind the counter at the station now."

"I want to be an artist," says Andy.

Jenny laughs. "Why do you question your life now?"

"I've been thinking about this for a long time," says Andy.

She laughs again. "You're born, you find a way to support yourself, and then you die."

"What about happiness?" he asks.

"Who said you have a right to be happy?" she asks. "Ask Benny."

"Benny, don't you want to be happy?" asks Andy, fishing for my support.

"Everyone wants to be happy." I wait for Jenny's angry eye.

"Not everyone can afford to be happy," she says.

Jenny stops talking when Joanna walks in the restaurant. I check my watch and see it's only three in the afternoon.

"Sorry, the immigration officer wants to have the last meeting tonight. We have to go."

Jenny shakes her head. "Go."

"Thank you, Jenny," I say.

"You still owe me ten thousand dollars," she says.

"I'm aware. And I'm grateful you're giving me time to pay it off."

"Come back right after, we're short-handed," says Jenny.

The immigration officer arrives promptly at five. I quickly offer him a seat because my legs are shaky. If we are found out, Joanna will go to prison and I will be deported. I won't be able to return. All this suffering would have been in vain. The worst part would be letting down Betty and my son.

He asks us about our future plans while Joanna and I hold hands. We are asked many of the same questions from our first interview: where we met, our favorite meal, which side of the bed we sleep on. Joanna squeezes my hand and I squeeze back. Years of practice make us look like a couple. After an hour of questioning, he gets up.

"I enjoyed meeting you both. Good luck to you." I walk him to the door and shake his hand.

I close the door and lean up against it. "It's over," I whisper.

"I'm going to look for houses tomorrow. Do you want to come?"

"Jenny is not going to let me off on a Saturday." I walk away but she keeps questioning me.

"How will I know what you want?" she asks.

"I'm not going with you," I say.

"Where will you go?" she asks. Her pale eyes fill with tears. She is hoping I'll keep her company in the new house.

"I need to get a place ready for Betty and my son," I tell her. Joanna is silent, as if someone has punched her in the throat. A small gasp of air escapes her and she bolts out of the room. I feel sorry for her. I think if I was free to be with someone, perhaps I could grow to love Joanna. Her heart is big, and she gives it freely. I hope she finds someone who deserves her.

I try to call Betty to ask her to marry me, but her phone number is no longer working. I've asked a friend to check on her. He says no one answers the door.

I place an extra offering to Buddha. I pray Betty and my son are alright.

I pray all their dreams come true.

Candyland

I'm happy to be out of our dark apartment. Our lights are turned off again. It seems like only the bugs can find their way around our smelly home. Mami says they're called roaches. Our neighbor calls the stink mold. She claims it will kill us, but it doesn't seem to affect the bugs.

I break away from Mami and run up and down the aisles. I twirl around in the dress the pastor's wife gave to us. It flows like waves as I jump around between other people's grocery carts.

The colorful displays catch my eye. I want the crayons so much, but I pull my hand back from the boxes. Mami says I'm almost nine and I should know we don't touch things we can't buy.

"Jessica, come." She gives me a quick glance and marches to the cash register. She said we can only buy a couple of things we need for the next few days. A rainstorm is coming, and we have to hurry because we have a hard walk home. The grocery store on Buford Highway isn't far from our apartment, but dodging cars on the side of the road is bad enough on a sunny day.

She gives me the look that has two meanings—*stop what you're doing* and *get your behind over here*. I run to catch up to her.

The cashier winks at me. I keep staring at her until Mami pokes me in the back.

The woman rings up the cans of Spam, a loaf of bread, and some things that don't need to be cooked. Mami winces like I do when I know Papi is going to spank me. She only has a few dollars my Papi gave her before he left for a construction job in Alabama. He promised more money after he gets back but Mami said he will probably be cheated again.

"What choice do we have?" he always says before he climbs into the back of a stranger's pickup truck. Most times, we don't know where he's going.

We had all the food we wanted back home. Our real home. I'm not allowed to say where. Papi owned a restaurant. After school, I'd go visit him and he'd bring out plates of bread, roasted meat, and sweet sodas.

I look over at the candy and gum next to the counter. I can't believe all the choices. I lick my lips and turn to Mami for her approval but she doesn't notice me. Her eyes are glued to the cash register. My head turns to the cashier then back to Mami then back to the cashier as if I'm watching an out-of-control bouncing ball. Even though it's never happened before, I hope there will be some coins left so I can have a little treat.

Mami shakes her head slightly and grits her teeth. She grabs my hand. She gives me the *don't embarrass me* look.

The cashier tells Mami the total. Mami's eyes well up. She looks like a popped balloon, with her shoulders hanging low. Her hands shake and she points at the can of tuna, smoked sausages, peanut butter, and strawberry jam.

"Not the jam," I blurt out. I'm ashamed of saying it out loud. Mami squeezes my shoulder. I wonder if it's because she's trying to comfort me or because I embarrassed her. Secretly, I'm glad we're not taking the tuna. It smells awful. I hope Mami doesn't see it in my face. I'm ashamed again because it's my father's favorite and he should have it when he comes home.

The cashier gives her the new total and Mami hands her a small paper sack of coins. After the cashier counts out the money, she smiles, and points to the candy rack. Mami pulls me closer to her and shakes her head. The cashier takes some change out of her own pocket and throws it into the cash register. She reaches over and grabs a pack of gum.

Mami waves her hands so fast that I start getting nervous too. Her lips move but nothing comes out. I've never seen

Mami cry or even come close to it.

"What's your name?" the cashier asks me as she snaps her gum.

I'm too afraid to answer.

"My name is Soon Yi," she tells us.

We don't answer.

Soon Yi walks around the register, takes Mami's hands, puts the pack of gum inside and closes them. She pats Mami on the shoulder and they look at each other.

"I know what you're going through. Take it before my manager comes out."

"Say thank you," Mami tells me.

"Grac . . . thanks," I say.

As Mami and I get to the door, we turn back to look at our new friend. She smiles and waves at us. I try to wave back but she starts helping the next customer in line.

I run to catch up to Mami.

Donor Number 2000-799

All the years Sandy waited to be filled with life, I knew I was only injecting her with emptiness. I went along on her quest to have children, thinking she would eventually give up. Over the years, she completed countless fertility tests, researched adoption agencies, and joined a surrogacy group. And worse, she hoped.

Sitting in Sandy's latest fertility clinic, I squeeze her hand. I study the floor to avoid looking at her. Only when she touches my thigh do I stop tapping my foot.

After the last test had concluded she was fertile, she'd pushed me into having tests of my own. I'd hoped the doctor would tell her I didn't have any working sperm left. My senior year of college, I'd tried to donate sperm. The sperm donation center's director sat me down and explained my sperm's increasingly low motility. Being twenty-two years old, I shrugged it off. In my mind, I would deal with it later.

The doorknob turns and I jump out of the chair. The doctor slides into the office and shakes his head.

"Please sit," he says.

"Is it bad news?" asks Sandy.

"Have you discussed the alternatives we spoke about at our last visit? There are other ways. You could adopt. You could use a sperm donor." Dr. Weinstein offers several pamphlets.

"Oh, there's no chance for us?" she asks.

Sandy looks at me, but I stare straight ahead, studying the diplomas on the doctor's walls. I try to stand but Sandy tugs at my shirt.

"Let's hear him out," says Sandy.

"I'm done." I push the pamphlets away from me and walk out.

"I'm sorry," I hear Sandy say to Dr. Weinstein.

"I understand, dear. Give it some time." Dr. Weinstein's voice gets smaller as I escape down the hallway.

Sandy chases me to the parking lot. "Why did you leave? This is nothing to be ashamed of. A lot of couples do it."

"I can't," I say, opening the car door. "I just can't."

I'm grateful Sandy is silent all the way home. I know she's angry, but I can't get into it with her now. I stop the car outside our building. Sandy had felt this place would bring us better luck so we had waited a year for a condo to open up at this prestigious Peachtree Street address.

"I have to get back to work. Are you going to be okay?" I still can't look at her.

"Yes." Sandy slams the door.

I drive off before she decides to get back in the car.

A FEW MONTHS ago, I had caught the beginning of a documentary about sperm donors. One of the donors found out he had one hundred and fifty children. The doctor had promised him there would be no more than six children per donor, but greed prevailed.

My head swirled. I wondered how many of my children were out there. Curiosity about the children had pulled at me now and then. I hadn't had time to write down the name of the donor registry because Sandy had walked into the room. I'd quickly changed the channel to her favorite show, *Modern Family*.

After eight hours of sitting at my desk and thinking about how to avoid Sandy, I come home to an empty house. Relieved, I hurry into my office, and lock the door. I Google "sperm donor," and after a few minutes, I find the donor registry.

I pause. What if someone contacts me? The website assures all inquiries will be kept confidential. That gives me a slight level of reassurance.

Holding my breath, I click on the link. They only need two pieces of information—the name of the sperm bank, and the donor number. Allendale Clinic. Enter. 2000-799. Enter. The donor number was the first year their sperm was donated, and the donor's personal identification code.

The home screen appears, and I open up the chat room. Their parents had signed up to allow their children to meet their siblings. The children are calling each other "diblings," slang for donor siblings. I can't breathe. It's too much to digest in one sitting. It's incomprehensible. What I exchanged for seventy dollars a donation turned into human beings.

Each child has a link. I click on several pages. There are the photos I wanted to see and much more. The videos play sounds of laughter, cooing, talking. I'm mesmerized by first steps, falling off bikes, and birthday parties.

One of the links is marked "Urgent." Do I really want to see it? I've come this far. How can I stop now?

I click on the link and see a beautiful girl dressed in a bouncy, pink dress.

I click on the video. A woman smiles, pauses, and wipes a tear from her cheek.

"Hi, my name is Jenna. I have breast cancer. My daughter is six years old. I don't have any relatives. I don't know where to turn." She pauses as the camera turns to the girl.

I stop the video, breathing in deeply. I try to collect myself and resume listening to her plea.

"It would be wonderful if one of the dibling families adopted her. I don't want her to grow up in foster care." She puts her hands over her face, but her tears flowed through her fingers.

"I will ask my wife," a concerned father comments.

"I will pray for you," is repeated several times by other parents.

"We're all family, and will always be bonded," is the last entry.

I try to close the page, but my hands are trembling. I shiver. Images of my mother, long buried, swirl inside my head. She tried so hard to hide her pain. "I will always love you, Jake. Someday, when you have children of your own, you will know there is no love greater than between parent and child."

I dial the number at the bottom of the page.

"Hello?" Jenna's voice is barely audible.

"Mommy, who is it?" asks a squeaky voice.

I pull the phone away from my ear and begin to hang up.

"Sorry, hello?" she asks.

"Umm, hi. I saw your page on the registry."

"Oh, yes, are you a dibling parent?" she asks.

"No, not exactly," I say.

"Who are you?" she asks.

"I'm the fa . . . I'm donor number 2000-799."

"Oh." The second of silence seems to go on forever.

"Mommy, mommy, let me talk," says the smaller voice.

"Just a minute, Danielle," she says in a weakened voice.

I sit back in my chair. Danielle.

"Sorry, what did you say your name was?" she asks.

"I apologize. Jake. Jake Elliot." Danielle's mother falls silent again.

"My name is Jenna. My daughter is . . ."

"Danielle. I heard. That was my mother's name."

"Oh," Jenna says again.

"Beautiful name. That's what I would name a girl if I had one." I smack myself on the forehead. I've said too much.

"Jake, I'm feeling a little sick tonight. Could we speak tomorrow?"

"Yes, of course."

DAYS PASS WHILE I go through the motions at work and at home. I berate myself for opening the door. Why did I call? What will I tell Sandy?

Jenna finally calls me. "The clinic verified your name. Do you want to talk?"

"Sure, tomorrow?" I ask before thinking.

"Do you know where Caribou Coffee is on North Highland? Can you meet there tomorrow morning, around ten?"

"I look forward to it. See you then." I slide my phone into a drawer. I can't talk to anyone else today.

THE NEXT MORNING, I arrive at the coffee shop at nine. I need time to gather myself before I meet the mother of my child. Shortly after ten, I notice Jenna moving slowly down the sidewalk. I run over to meet her.

"Hi, Jenna?" I ask as I offer my hand.

"Jake, it's nice to meet you," she says and stumbles.

I hold her up by the shoulders, steadying her.

"I'm sorry. The weakness comes and goes so suddenly." She blushes.

"My mother had cancer." I put out my arm and she holds onto me until we reach a chair inside the coffee shop.

Jenna smiles. "Can we just get to it?"

I nod. "Of course."

"What made you search for her?" asks Jenna.

"I was curious. And I came across your page. I apologize if I invaded your privacy."

"No need. This is quite new for both of us." She looks down at the table.

"What does she know about me?" I ask.

"Nothing. She's a bit young. I always planned on telling her when she was older."

"I know what it's like to be alone after your mother dies." I follow the grooves in the table with my index finger.

"How does your wife feel about all this?" she asks.

"My wife?" My eyes widen.

"Your ring," she says.

"I haven't told her yet. I didn't know if anything would come of this. We're having fertility issues. I didn't want to upset her." I close my eyes. I've said too much again.

"Maybe this is too much responsibility for you," she says.

"Maybe it is. But I want to meet Danielle."

"How about 3:00 tomorrow? Danielle will be back from school then." Jenna waits for my answer.

"Okay, I'll see you then." I wonder what I'll tell Sandy about where I'm going. "Can I give you a lift home?"

"No, the doctor said I should try to exercise a bit. And it'll give me time to think about what to tell Danielle."

THE NEXT DAY, I drive by their craftsman style house several times. The fourth time I pass by, I notice Jenna peeking out her lace curtains. I park on the street, thinking it too intimate to park in her driveway. Jenna cracks open the thin, yellow door. It seems too heavy for her.

"Hello, please come in," Jenna says. "She's here, but she's trying on all her dresses. We haven't had a visitor in a while."

Danielle bolts out of her bedroom door. "Hi! Mommy said we're going for ice cream."

"Yes, anywhere you want," I tell her.

"Mommy! He said anywhere I want." Danielle grins. "I got my school pictures today. Do you want to see them?"

"That would be great." I wipe my forehead with the back of my hand.

Danielle pulls a large, white envelope out of her backpack. "Look, Mommy said I'm the prettiest girl in the world."

"Yes, you are," I confirm.

"Do you want something to drink?" Jenna asks.

I wonder if she has any alcohol. "Water please."

Danielle runs over to the bookcase and points to a photo album. "Can you get that down? I have to put my picture in it." I pull down the album and hand it to Danielle.

Jenna returns with a glass of water.

"Thank you."

Danielle sits on Jenna's lap and giggles. "Tell him about the pictures."

"This is her first birthday. That's her first step." She continues to flip through the years.

"This is my first day of school," Danielle announces.

"I'm sorry. This is too much." Jenna sits back in her chair.

"Are you okay?" I ask.

"Danielle, why don't you finish getting dressed and then we can go get ice cream."

"But . . ." Danielle crosses her arms and pouts.

"Go on, I need to speak to Mr. Jake." She smiles lovingly at her daughter.

"Okay," Danielle says as she trudges to her bedroom.

Jenna shivers slightly, pulling a blanket over her shoulders.

"What are your intentions? I don't have that much time. Some of the other families want her." Jenna stops to catch her breath.

"I don't know . . ." I'm still holding Danielle's school photo in my hand.

"I thought she would be happier with blood relatives. I grew up in foster care. I always wanted a family of my own. Now she'll be alone like I was." Jenna's body rocks as she tries to contain her tears.

Danielle runs back into the living room. "Can we go now?"

"She is excited about leaving the house. I haven't been able to take her anywhere for a while."

Once settled in the car, I watched Danielle from the rearview mirror. She sings a song to herself then giggles.

"Are you Mommy's boyfriend?" she asks.

My face warms. "What do you know about boyfriends?"

"Jeffrey is my boyfriend at school. He said he's going to marry me. Are you going to marry Mommy?"

Jenna's cheeks turn pink this time. The color seems to

bring her back to life.

"I'm married already," I tell her.

When we reach the ice cream shop, Jenna gives Danielle a quarter. "Go get a toy from the machine and let the grown-ups talk."

"Yay!" Danielle bolts to the vending machines.

"Jake, I'm sorry. I was being unfair to you back at the house." Jenna pats my shoulder.

I place my hands in my pockets and rock back and forth on my heels.

"Maybe we should meet a few more times before you make a decision. And you could bring Sandy next time."

Danielle comes back to us and grabs my hand. "I want a sundae with whipped cream and sprinkles."

"Anything you want," I tell her.

Jenna and Danielle both nod.

OTHER THAN THE cordial "hellos" and questions about dinner, Sandy and I haven't spoken about our future. She's looked at me, staring, waiting for me to say something. But I have ignored her.

"We have to talk," Sandy says as I try to scoot past her. "I don't understand why you won't talk about our other options for having kids. You were so happy when your cousin adopted their baby. You threw a baby shower for the neighbors when their surrogate delivered their son. You always seemed so understanding."

She reaches out to me but I turn and go to my office to get my laptop. I go to the registry website and then hand the computer to her.

"This is what I've been doing. I'm so sorry for hiding it. I just didn't know how to tell you."

Her eyes widen as they wash over the screen. "What the hell is this? Have you been donating sperm? I thought you were having an affair, watching porn, anything but this."

"I did it a million years ago." I shift feet, unable to stand still.

"All these kids? They're yours?" Sandy's face tightens for a moment then tears spill down her face. "You gave it all away!" Her cheeks become dark as ripe plums.

"I'm sorry. It was before I met you."

She shakes her head.

"I have been meeting with Danielle, my . . . and her mother."

"Say it! Your daughter."

"Her mother has cancer. She wants us to adopt Danielle." I blurt it out. I don't have the words to cushion the blow.

"Are you considering it?" Sandy looks at me through a flood of tears.

"I wanted to ask you what you thought. We were going to adopt anyway."

"But she would be yours, not mine." The laptop falls out of Sandy's hands and crashes on the floor.

"Does the clinic have any more sperm? We could try to have our own baby." Her words gush out.

"No, I won't do that," I tell her.

"Why?"

"It seems wrong to start another life when one that already exists needs us. Will you meet her?" I rub her arms. "Can you . . ."

"Are you crazy?" Sandy runs into the bathroom and slams the door.

I touch the doorknob but think twice about forcing the door open. With the barrier between us, I feel safer telling her the truth.

"I needed the money. In my mind, it didn't make a family. Then you came along. You had such a different background than I did. I couldn't tell you. It was too painful, and I didn't want to lose you."

"All this time, I thought it was me. My own mother said it

was my fault. She's been throwing the fact that Shane's wife is pregnant in my face."

"No one can measure up to your brother in your mother's eyes. You know that."

"And surely this won't help."

"I'm sorry. Can you forgive me?"

"Just go away," Sandy yells through the door.

After hours of pleading with Sandy to come out of the bathroom, I pack a bag and check into the Westin hotel. My calls, texts, and emails go unanswered for weeks.

JENNA ASKS ME if I really want Danielle. She needs a decision quickly, as her doctor told her she probably won't live to see next summer. Preparations will have to be made to ready Danielle for the transition.

Three donor families have stepped forward to take Danielle. The best option is one that has an eight-year old girl from one of my donations. They want a sibling for their own daughter and are ready to make Danielle a part of their family.

I sit on a park bench at Piedmont Park and watch Danielle twirl around in the sequined, purple dress I bought for her. I pull out my phone. Still nothing from Sandy. I bow my head and take in a deep breath.

Danielle waves. To her, I'm more than Donor Number 2000-799.

Photograph

practice my smile in the rear-view mirror before I meet my client, Roseanne Lawrence. Rumor is Roseanne is an heir-ess—tin or copper or something. We met several times at a nearby coffee shop before she deemed me worthy to pass through her hand-forged security gates.

Her assistant, Mollie, instructs me to wait in the foyer as I try to balance my heavy equipment. "Mrs. Lawrence will show you where to set up."

I attempt to set down the cameras.

"No. No. You can't put those on the marble floor. It's just been polished." She turns white and shakes her head. "Wait for Mrs. Lawrence."

"How long will she be?" I ask.

Roseanne appears at the top of her double spiral staircase. "Susie, it is lovely to see you again," she says. She glides down the stairs as if she's Miss America.

My name is Suzanne, but I have learned over the years not to correct the rich. If they say your name is Susie, it's Susie, even if your birth certificate doesn't agree.

"Mrs. Lawrence, thank you for inviting me to your beautiful home." I extend my right hand, holding on to the camera and tripod with my left arm.

She nods and walks away.

My face burns. I don't know why I keep smiling even after she leaves the room.

"Are you joining me?" asks Roseanne from the other room. She lets out a pronounced sigh as if I'm holding up her process.

"Yes, I'm coming."

Her children, Baxter and Grace, are corralled in front of the fireplace, which Roseanne points out was brought over from a Tuscan villa. Dressed in custom-made clothes designed by a protégé of Ralph Lauren, they plop themselves on the chairs. Arms crossed and faces downturned, they refuse to cooperate.

"Hands in your laps, backs straight, smile," I say in a sing-song voice.

Nothing. The littlest one crosses her eyes and sticks her tongue out at me. I'm tempted to take the shot. How great would that portrait look over their precious mantle?

"Smile. Look here!" I snap. Nothing. I clap. Nothing. My voice hits a high note that possibly only their well-coiffed dog can hear.

I glance at Roseanne for assistance, but she looks at me flatly as if to say *I'm paying you to deal with this.* After more eye-pleading from me, Roseanne claps her hands together.

"Make Mommy happy and you will get the new iPad Airs tomorrow." Roseanne leans toward them, other words are exchanged. The rich also whisper in inaudible tones that the rest of us can't hear.

Their little faces snap into submission. Their painted-on smiles beam with confidence as if to say *I will rule the world one day.*

I stare at them until Roseanne clears her throat and taps her Cartier watch with her manicured index finger.

"Wonderful," I say to break the awkwardness.

Roseanne puts her hands on her hips.

"Look how pretty you are, Grace. Wow, Baxter. You are so handsome." I know I sound ridiculous, but compliments always help the process. I take typical sibling portraits and their in-dividual poses. They periodically have to be reprimanded by Roseanne.

Thirty minutes into the session, Grace lets out a mini-sigh. Roseanne smiles with gritted teeth, smooths out her Tory Burch dress, and lets out a grown-up sigh.

"Are we done?" She sighs again. "The children have piano

lessons."

I chuckle for no apparent reason. "They were perfect."

"Okay, then Mollie will show you out." Roseanne struts out of the room without Grace and Baxter.

"Olga!" she yells from the foyer.

A gray-haired woman appears from the hallway with mugs of hot chocolate, overflowing with giant marshmallows.

"Hello, I'm Olga. It's nice to meet you."

"My name is Suzanne," I say as I round up my cameras.

Olga takes a tray of hot cocoa over to the children. "Drink."

"It's too hot!" Grace screams. She throws herself, face down, into the ottoman.

Olga winks at me and says, "The helplessness starts at an early age."

Mollie returns, helps round up my equipment, and practically pushes me to the door. "Please call me when the portraits are completed." She closes the door in my face before I have a chance to respond.

I'm on the expressway before I realize my plastered smile is still on my face. I open my mouth to unclench my jaw. I remind myself I'm not in their world anymore—no mansion, no servants, no made-up annoyances.

The apartment I grew up in could fit in Roseanne's foyer. Our small, mold-infested space didn't house any photos. Mother couldn't afford school pictures, let alone a camera. After diapers, generic brand foods, and clothes from Goodwill, we were in the hole every month.

Every September, as my classmates exchanged autographed pictures of themselves, I hid in the library and cried. My best friend, Megan, brought her Polaroid camera to school one year and offered to take a special picture of me. She waved the square back and forth to develop the photo then presented it.

"So you'll always remember what you looked like," she told me. "Take the camera. Maybe you can take more pictures if you don't like this one."

I have little left of my childhood, but I kept the photo and camera. When I least expect it, the photo slips out of a drawer or a book. I'm not smiling. I wonder how the sad girl with tattered clothing, frazzled hair, and Kool-Aid-stained lips became a photographer for the rich.

I still don't smile, unless it's to demonstrate to the wealthy children how it's done. The little bastards always refuse until they are properly bribed by their parents. Sometimes I think they're manipulating their parents for larger gifts. Sometimes I think they sense I don't know what a real smile is. Even with all their wealth, I don't think they're any happier than I was at their age.

Driving home from Roseanne's house in my usual trance, I see the homeless girl again. I'm not sure what makes me stop the car this time. I've seen hundreds of panhandlers on my commute to and from my clients' homes, but it hasn't affected me before.

The frail, blonde girl stands on the Lost Mountain Road off ramp. Her sign reads, "My baby needs food and diapers." Several passengers in the cars ahead of me hand her folded bills. I park the car halfway onto the shoulder and walk over to her.

"Can I give you a lift somewhere?" The girl shakes her head. She's much younger than she appears from a distance.

"No ma'am. We don't have anywhere to go." She rubs her baby's head.

"Let me take you to the store and buy you a few things." I reach out for her hand.

"It's okay," she says. She turns her baby away from me and takes a step back. The baby looks up and smiles, unaffected by their circumstances.

"It's going down to forty-five degrees tonight. Where will you sleep?"

The girl glances briefly at the bushes behind the directional signs. When she catches me looking at her, she looks away.

"We'll be okay."

"Well, let me give you something for the baby." I go back to my car and return with a blanket I use for outdoor shoots.

"Thank you." The girl wraps the blanket around herself and her baby.

"Take care." I force myself not to look back as I walk away.

I watch them from my rearview mirror as I exit onto the main road. I coast about a half mile toward my house then decide I can't leave her there. Making a U-turn, I park the car in the grass near the end of the off-ramp.

My heels sink into the dirt shoulder as I make it back to the girl. She watches me approach and holds her baby tighter.

"I'm not going to hurt you. Would you like to stay at my house tonight?"

"No, I told you we'd be okay." She takes another step back.

"It's not safe out here."

"I've heard," she says.

"Just one night. I'll take you to the shelter tomorrow." I hold out my hand, waiting for her to take it.

Two male panhandlers stop a few feet from us.

"Okay," says the girl.

"My name is Suzanne." I put myself between her and the two men.

"I'm Melanie, and this is Jane." She studies the men carefully.

"Good. Let's go. It'll be dark soon. Why don't we stop at the store and get some formula and diapers?"

"Thank you." Melanie frowns, pulls the blanket over her baby's face as we pass the men and walk to my car.

WHEN WE ARRIVE at the house, my husband is preparing dinner. He looks up from the cutting board and notices the unexpected guest.

"Are you going to join us for dinner?" he asks the stranger while staring at me.

"They're going to stay with us for a while," I say.

"Okay then, I'll throw a couple more chicken breasts on the grill," he says.

"Thanks," says Melanie, fidgeting as if she's waiting for an introduction.

"Hi, I'm Adam, Suzanne's husband." He waves at her.

"I'm Melanie, and this is Jane." Melanie grips Jane tighter.

Adam doesn't notice the baby until Melanie announces it. He leaves the vegetables on the cutting board and drifts over to the duo.

"Hey there," he says as he squeezes Jane's cheeks.

"He likes kids," I say.

"Why don't you get them settled? I'll finish dinner." Adam goes back to his preparations as I guide Melanie out of the kitchen.

"Do you have kids?" she asks me.

"No," I whisper.

"Sorry," she says and looks away.

"Here is the guest room and bath. Let me know if you need anything else. I can send Adam to the store."

"Thank you." Melanie closes the door slowly behind her, but I stand on the other side asking myself if I have done the right thing by bringing her to the house.

I dread going back downstairs. Adam grew up in an upper middle-class family. How could he understand Melanie's situation?

"Where did you find that girl?" he demands.

"Shhh . . . she'll hear you." I put my finger to my lips.

"She's filthy," he says.

"Homeless." I move to the cabinet and take out three plates.

"What if she robs us? Or kills us."

"Don't be so paranoid. I couldn't let them sleep on the street."

"You don't even like children," he informs me.

"Yes, I do." I breathe slowly and deeply waiting for his

interrogation to end.

"Well, you never wanted any," he says.

"I can't have them. I'm barren. Is that what you want to hear?" I slam the plates on the kitchen table.

"Sorry we took so long," says Melanie. She stands in the doorway with Jane on her hip.

"No problem," says Adam. He places the pre-measured chicken, wild rice, and green beans on each plate. "Come, sit."

Melanie studies the three items that don't touch each other.

"Is there something wrong? If you want more, please don't hesitate to ask."

"No, it's just that it's so pretty." Melanie's eyes well up.

"I guess it is." Adam stares out the window while he takes a sip of water.

"Please start," I say, trying to put Melanie at ease.

Melanie stands up. "Let me fix a bottle for Jane."

"Oh, we forgot." Adam and I jump up. We hardly ever eat at the kitchen table. We usually take our plates to separate corners of the house—Adam to his office, and I to my studio. Thinking about guests, especially a baby, is beyond us.

"Can you just show me where . . ." She scans the kitchen.

Adam runs ahead of Melanie. "Yes, of course." I watch them as they prepare Jane's bottle together.

THE ONE NIGHT Melanie and Jane were supposed to stay with us has turned into a month. Adam has really taken to them. I hear him telling Melanie she and Jane can stay as long as they like. He's been making organic baby food almost on a daily basis.

I've taken a break from my job, no longer able to fake my way through the day. I can't force myself to stomach people like Roseanne. It seems her only desire is to produce the life-size photographs of her heirs that she can hang in her grand hallway. They will always remember what they looked like as children—or rather, what their mother staged them to be.

When the portraits are ready, I call Mollie and tell her I had a stomach virus. I tell her I don't want to infect the children but, in truth, I don't want to go back there. She echoes my excuses to Roseanne.

"Oh yes, the children. Just have the portraits delivered to us." She repeats what Roseanne says then hangs up.

I spend the rest of the morning taking pictures of Melanie and Jane. They are wearing the matching dresses Adam bought for them. Melanie smiles without prodding. She bounces Jane, and Jane giggles.

As the pair play at the park, I make them a keepsake. I present the leather-bound album to Melanie. She opens the brass clasp and flips through it slowly. She begins to smile then tells me she can't take it with her. It's too heavy for her to lug around from shelter to shelter.

Even after I beg, Melanie tells me she can't stay. I understand she needs a foundation of her own. I tell her I'll hold on to the album for her until she gets settled somewhere. It will always be here if Jane wants to see her baby pictures or if Melanie wants to see herself young again. She nods, but I know she won't be back.

She takes down the old Polaroid camera from my bookshelf. She asks if I will take a picture of them with it. One square photo is easily tucked inside a bag, easily transported.

"I don't know if it still has film," I say. She laughs and lifts Jane to the sky. The sequins in Jane's dress sparkle. Both mother and daughter cackle, and I take the shot.

Melanie takes the camera from me and places Jane in my arms. I feel my cheeks redden.

"It's your turn," she says.

"No, I don't look good in pictures," I plead. "And I'm not properly dressed."

"You look perfect. Please, I want to be able to show Jane what you look like."

I reluctantly oblige, hoping Melanie will remember me as

someone other than the angry woman in the photo. She takes two photos.

Adam offers to drop them off at the women's shelter in Cartersville, thirty miles north of us. He knows I don't like drawn-out farewells and I assume he wants to spend a little more time with Jane.

As I watch them drive away, I see the Polaroid Melanie took of me on my desk.

I pick it up.

I'm finally smiling.

Job Search

I've been looking for a job for three months now. You'd think there would be plenty of positions in Atlanta. Dozens of companies are relocating here. There are thousands of job postings on CareerBuilder, Monster, LinkedIn.

I also have five recruiters looking on my behalf. One of them tells me there is an opening at a megachurch on 10th Street.

"It's perfect for you," says Tiffani. She throws her arms up as if her football team scored a goal.

I tell her I'd rather not work at another church. I need a change.

"Elise, what are your skills? What makes you stand out from the other ninety-nine applicants who will apply for the same position?" Tiffani waits for my response.

I'm really good at taking pictures of people while hiding behind cars and bushes. I'm good at knowing and reporting what people wish to keep private. I'm good at ignoring a good woman who needs help. I'm good at being a bad person.

Of course, none of these qualities will help me get a job.

"I can type sixty words per minute," I say.

"Are you bilingual?"

"No."

"Are you proficient in Excel?"

"No."

"Can you work a ten-line phone?"

"No."

Tiffani rolls her eyes. "Why don't we change the layout of your resumé? Use power words like strategic, proactive, hit the ground running."

Now I roll my eyes.

"It's just a suggestion." She closes the folder. "Well okay, I'll let you know if something comes up." She shows me to the door.

The indignity of job searching as a middle-aged, overweight, and under-skilled woman slaps me in the face every single day. Without references, it's almost impossible to get a job even at a fast food restaurant or discount retail store. My boss—former boss—ran away from the church where I worked. He can't do anything for me now.

I'm fifty-two years old. Four out of the five managers I've interviewed with were younger than I am. I suppose I'll have to report to someone half my age.

A real estate company calls me for an interview. I helped manage the church's buildings but since I don't have a real estate license, I'm told this position starts at twenty-eight thousand dollars a year. At this point, I'd take it. The credit card companies are threatening legal action. My car is paid off, but I can't afford to fix the air conditioning.

The junior vice president invites me to lunch rather than to his office. He brags about his big house in the suburbs, his wife, and his kids. After half an hour, he starts questioning me.

"Is there a reason you couldn't work overtime if required?" he asks.

"No, I can work late." I watch him wolf down his grilled bison salad without dressing. "No dressing," he'd repeated twice to the waiter.

"So, no boyfriend, husband, kids?"

I shake my head.

"Coolio," he says and laughs. "Coolio used to be a rapper when my parents were teenagers," he explains then laughs again.

He calls two weeks later and tells me he "went in a different direction." In other words, younger. Someone more Coolio.

One of my recruiters comes through and sets up an interview at a delivery company. I meet three different managers on three different days over a two-week period. They all ask me the same questions. They all tell me I'm qualified.

The human resources director glances at my resumé and notices I graduated from South Cobb High School. "Hey, I graduated there in 2004. What year did you graduate?"

I never hear back from them.

A rep from an insurance company finds my resumé on a job board. A man calls and asks, "Now, tell me if this is too personal. We just want to see how you would handle conflict. Do you fight with your husband, and how do you resolve it?"

I just hang up the phone.

I find a part-time job posting on Craigslist. It's for Books & Brews, a coffee shop and bookstore in town. It's owned by a gay man named Howard Frank. When it first opened, my boss organized a rally and book burning. The store sold gay-themed fiction. For the church, that was way up there on the sin meter.

The boycott lasted a couple of days. Then the picketers had to get back to work. The Atlanta residents wanted good coffee. Readers wanted to support local bookstores.

I was there. I was the church's representative. Would Mr. Frank recognize me? I've always blended into the background.

He greets me in his Kate Bush t-shirt and tattered jeans. "Hi, please take a seat."

I look for recognition in his eyes.

"Do you have any experience making coffee drinks?"

"No."

"Have you ever run a cash register?"

"No."

"Ever worked retail?"

"No."

"Can you get here around 4:30 in the morning? We open up the store at five."

"Yes. Do you want to see my resumé?"

"What does a piece of paper tell you about anyone? I hire people I like, people who my customers will like."

"Oh, I'll go then."

"Come back at 4:30 tomorrow. My assistant manager will show you the ropes."

"Really? You're hiring me?"

"Sure, but we won't be burning any books tomorrow."

Howard winks at me.

Change

I take the coins from my daughter Bailey's hand, making sure there is enough for a candy bar and soda. I close my eyes, imagining the salty caramel and soft, sweet chocolate swirling around in my mouth.

"Thank you for coming," I tell her.

I hold the money from Bailey's allowance—mostly nickels and dimes. Some are sticky and stained as if she found them on the street. They are still warm from her soft hands. I place the small bundle of change in my pocket, patting it down to make sure it doesn't suddenly disappear.

"I brought a copy of my check-writing homework," Bailey tells me. She lays the paper on the table and waits for me to sit so we can begin our lesson.

I'm struck by how much she has grown since I saw her. She has a sweet smell to her, like from a fancy shampoo or body mist. Her pink cardigan and khaki skirt are freshly pressed. Her loafers are shiny, not scuffed up like the other shoes she inherited after her four sisters had their turn in them.

I look down at my jeans and sweatshirt. Thankfully, they are clean.

"Mom?"

I sit across from her at the small table in the visitors' area.

"Ready?" she asks.

I nod.

"The payee is who receives the check. Here is where you put the date. Here, you write the numbers. Here, you write out the amount." She pauses as if she's unsure of my capabilities.

I write slowly, hoping not to disappoint her.

"And no change," says Bailey, pressing her index finger on the blank spot where I have forgotten part of her instructions.

I nod.

"Don't forget to put the two small zeros above the one hundred," Bailey says. "That's the change."

This time, I placed a "50" above the one hundred. "That's a little bit of change."

We both attempt to smile.

When Bailey learned how to write checks in her seventh-grade math class, I'd asked her to teach me. I'd never made it that far in school. Even if I had, there never would have been enough money to open up a bank account. Before I met Freddie, my husband, drugs or alcohol took the money well before the bank could. After we got married, he took whatever tips I made at the strip club.

"The social worker told me you're doing really good in school," I say.

"Well. Well in school." Bailey corrects me. "I earned A's and B's."

This is the first time I have discussed grades with any of my daughters. The first four dropped out of school and I always assumed Bailey would do the same.

"She's just another girl who'll end up dancing at the club," Freddie told me. I believed him.

"You shouldn't blame yourself," Anne, the owner of Second Chances Halfway House, where I'm currently serving out the rest my sentence, constantly tells me. She assures me all I can do now is to try to make things right for my daughters. I have to admit it's hard not to kick myself for not seeing things, or just ignoring them. The girls blame Freddie for their shattered lives. But I suppose it's easier to do that now because he's dead.

My second oldest, Rita, has been charged with his murder. If she did it, she had a right, although she's the only one Freddie didn't force to dance. "She has a face only fit for counting money," he often said. "She'd scare away the customers if I put her on the stage."

During the investigation, the police found a bunker full

of drugs and guns under the club. Freddie had put the building in my name, without my knowing it, so I was arrested. Anne heard about my trial and asked her contacts to assist in my case. The charges were reduced from intent to sell to possession.

Natasha Leach, the pastor's wife at Southern Heaven Sanctuary, mentors the women here. She read about me in the paper and offered to help. The prison was overcrowded and the warden needed to let a few prisoners out. Mrs. Leach told him I wasn't a threat to anyone. On her recommendation, I was allowed to serve one year at a halfway house and then probation for the next ten years.

"Don't forget to sign the check," says Bailey.

"I'm sorry," I whisper.

"It's okay," she says. She starts to doodle in her notebook. I put my pencil down and look at the floor.

Anne walks by and places a plate of cookies and two glasses of milk on the table. She turns back and winks at me. She opened up Second Chances twenty-two years ago. She was a rising star in Hollywood. Two of her movies made over one hundred million dollars and she was nominated for best supporting actress at The Golden Globes. She was dubbed the next Julia Roberts by *People* magazine.

Rumor is she was dating the famous Yogi of Atlanta. He's a spiritual guru who showed up from some unknown European country. The tabloids said she drove drunk and smashed up her car one night. With his reputation for clean living, he couldn't be associated with her and dumped her. Anne stopped acting, went missing for a year, and reappeared in her hometown of Jonesboro. The Internet says she's younger than me. She seems older, much more mature than I am. You wouldn't recognize her now—gray hair pulled back in a ponytail, slightly chubby, and no makeup at all. No one would ever guess she was a starlet once.

I've always had a bad feeling about Yogi. Freddie lost a

large hand to him in one of the poker games at the club. So he gave Brandi, my oldest, to him. She left quietly as if living with a stranger seemed so much better than staying with us.

"Aunt Helen says I'll be going to a private school when I move to Chicago," says Bailey.

"The judge said moving in with her permanently would be the best thing for you," I tell her.

Bailey nods.

I haven't seen my sister since I got pregnant with Brandi. I was sixteen and she was fifteen. Twenty-five years is a long time, even for sisters who refuse to see each other. Our mother split from our father after I ran away from home. I'm not sure why she waited until then. She had to have known what was going on with us. My father wasn't allowed to see any of us kids after the divorce was finalized.

I never knew where Helen was until Bailey needed a responsible guardian. The courts tracked her down and she agreed to take her. They've been living in a temporary apartment until all the custody issues are settled.

None of Bailey's sisters can look after her. Brandi said she can't take her because Yogi wants all the attention on him. They don't have time to raise a child. Rita is still awaiting trial. The police picked her up shortly after Freddie was found dead. Sherry, my third girl, ran away. Remy, well, she's at peace now.

My hand shakes as I bring the glass of milk to my lips. How I wish it was whiskey. I suppose it's appropriate my mother named me after a drink. I don't think she meant any harm by calling me Ginny. What else could I have become except a bartender and a drunk?

I did more than pour drinks. I drank a few on and off the job. I've been fired from most of the bars in and around Atlanta. By the time I landed at Freddie's, I was strung out on five or six drugs, legal and prescribed, all while toting Brandi along.

Freddie says he gave me a chance. Or, as Brandi says, "He

saw a victim."

Brandi never blamed me for our circumstances. She was quiet, taking care of the other girls who came along. Growing up in the bar, seeing all the prostitution, drug dealing, and gambling, had to have broken all the girls.

"How are the other kids treating you at school?" I ask Bailey.

She shrugs. "It's okay. I'll be in Chicago soon. Friends are useless anyway. Isn't that what Daddy always told us?"

When Natasha and Anne heard who my husband was, they looked at each other. Freddie has broken about every law on the books, but he had enough dirt on cops, judges, even men of God, to keep him out of jail. Even Natasha's husband was afraid of him. I've seen Pastor Leach slink through the back of the club now and again. He first came to lead Freddie to God, but Freddie led him to hell instead.

I've known hell all my life. I worried the whole time Brandi was in my stomach. Helen said she heard babies from incest came out as monsters. My mother never told us about sex. The only sex we knew was what our father pushed into us.

Maybe that's why I ignored what Freddie was doing. That's the excuse I tell myself. Only when I was drunk did I even halfway believe it.

Anne asked me if I wanted to join Alcoholics Anonymous. I told her that was for people who were ready to be forgiven or saved. I was not ready for either. I would only be ready when Bailey was safe and happy in Chicago.

Bailey will take Helen's last name so Bailey wouldn't be a Bell like me or a Lard like Freddie. She will be a Peterson—a new name, a new life. No one can Google her and find out her mother went to prison, or that her sister committed suicide, or that her other sister killed her father. She could be pure, fresh, and brand new.

Helen suggested to the social worker that we cut off visitation all together after the adoption. I didn't disagree with her. I wrote Helen, telling her she is free to raise Bailey as she sees fit, anywhere she wants. I won't interfere.

THE SECURITY GUARD at Second Chances storms into the waiting room. "Time's up!"

My right eye twitches. My tongue swells with all the words I should have said, but never did. I stop my hand inches from Bailey's hand. I don't know how Bailey will react to my touch.

"Let's wrap it up," announces the guard.

I go around the table to Bailey. I want to tell her so many things. I want to promise her beautiful dreams I will never be able to give her.

Bailey smiles.

I dig into my pocket and pull out the change she gave me for the vending machine. I place the coins in her palm and clamp my hands around hers.

"Here, take this. Put this back in your piggy bank. It's for us. It's for our future." I wait for Bailey to push me off as she has always done.

Her eyes rise up from our hands. "That's big change," she says.

Clean Slate

I wanted to say I shredded the application to music school. It was really in stack "A"—A for applications, the first in the line of neatly ordered papers I couldn't bear to throw away. Sometimes I got up in the middle of the night and debated whether or not it belonged in stack "J"—J for Juilliard.

The townhouse overflowed with neat stacks down the stairs, hallways, and in nearly every room. Since our memories overtook the garage two years ago, my car has been parked outside. Even my treasured piano held stories that couldn't be disposed of yet.

When Mother was alive, she kept the house in pristine condition, washing down the tile and hardwoods at least once a day. The white carpet was vacuumed diagonally every time someone stepped on it. The dust mop wore out about every week or so from cleaning the ceiling and walls. If company ever came over, which was rare, she spent hours wiping down the couch where a stranger's scent may have penetrated her germ barrier.

The foyer houses a built-in shoe rack my mother installed when we moved in. As Koreans, we removed our shoes before entering the house. The exterminator who made it halfway up the first flight of stairs wearing muddy service boots was then chased back down the driveway. Mother cleaned the carpet over and over for weeks. The mud stain is barely visible, but the carpet is worn down from the vigorous scrubbing.

My hoarding was contained to my car and bedroom. Mother rarely needed a ride anywhere and left my car alone, but she entered my room from time to time to destroy my ordered life.

"You're a dirty girl," she would yell. "You're a stupid, dirty girl." Apparently, my hoarding wasn't ordered enough for her.

No matter how often she said it, the sting never went away. The only time she was quiet was when I played the piano. She made me dust the refurbished Steinway and clean it with a special polish she ordered from Austria, all before I could play a note. Oh, yes, and I was forced to wash my hands with Boraxo hand soap both before and after going through her cleaning regimen.

"Think about all I had to do to provide this for you. You will become rich and famous and take care of me." She followed me around while I completed her checklist.

"Sorry, Mother. I've offended you again. I will do better." I learned to beg and plead on my knees at a very early age, then vacuum the indents in the carpet immediately after.

She always slapped me afterwards. It seemed to make her feel better. As my skin and heart toughened, I stopped crying. She made me wash my face anyway.

"Play," she demanded after the cleaning was finished. Mother closed her accusatory eyes. The only sound in the house was created by my immaculate fingers.

She pushed me to go to Juilliard. Getting in would prove she had been a good mother, which was the biggest prize a Korean mother could achieve. "You will need a scholarship," she barked. "You must practice every minute of the day."

Each year, I missed the application date. *The application was lost in the mail, the quota was filled,* and *there aren't any scholarships this year.* She believed all my excuses.

When I was twenty years old, she got sick. She never told me what she had. When she started coughing up blood, I tried to talk to her about it but she refused. She never allowed me to accompany her to the doctor. Only when I received the death certificate did I see the words lung cancer. That's where I also saw her date of birth for the first time.

She was much younger than she'd said she was. Only sixteen years separated us. When she was sober, she never mentioned my father. But when she was drunk and stressed, she would say he raped her. No amount of soap could wash away that statement.

Growing up, we didn't talk about family. She withdrew at the mention of relatives, only said all men were evil. I shouldn't trust anyone except her.

This is hard to follow because I work at Books & Brews. It's a local bookstore and coffee shop. Working with the public is not going well. I should be grateful my boss hasn't fired me the thousand times I got on his or my co-worker's nerves.

I used to be the assistant manager. At first, Howard was pleased with my work. My attention to detail increased sales for a while. But staff morale went down and soon even the customers started complaining about me.

Every morning, I brought out the laminated checklist. I went down the sheet, ticking off each box. If an item wasn't done properly, I had to start over at number one. I wouldn't let the other employees help because no one could do it better than I could.

Our agreement was that I would open the store and Howard would close. He received calls from the nervous co-workers. If Howard had not stepped in, prep could have taken the entire day. Customers would be lined up way past opening time. If things weren't perfect, I couldn't open the door.

"She's scrubbing the sinks with a toothbrush again," whispered the head barista.

"She's re-mopping the floors," said the reference desk attendant.

Howard sat me down one day. He reached over to pat my hand, but I pulled back. The last time he tried to touch me resulted in an hour of hand washing. Eventually, he had to send me home.

"I like you but we need to talk," he started. He had been the first one to take time to understand my quirks.

"I'm sorry I let you down again," I said.

"No, you didn't let me down." He lowered his head and exhaled. "You're just screwing yourself. You don't want that, do you?"

I sat on top of my hands, hoping Howard didn't see the effects of the heavy bleach I'd been using on the walls.

"The staff wants me to fire you. Can we address therapy again?" Howard ran out of steam and stopped.

"Is that really necessary?"

I thought about the elementary school nurse who questioned my severely cracked fingertips. She gave me a bottle of medicated lotion, but I threw it away. Did she think I would use it after hundreds of people touched it? What if they stuck their fingers in the bottle?

"That's the deal. Go see someone or I have to let you go. You're making everyone nervous." He wiped his palms on his jeans. The imagined wet spots made me nauseous.

"I need some water," I said.

"I'd get it for you, but I know how it is," he said.

"I'll be right back." I took a plastic cup from the center of the stack and filled it with water I brought from home. Mother installed a triple filtration system right before she died. I put the water through a Brita filter as well. Howard used a filter at the shop, but it was only a one-step process.

Howard studied my cup. "Well, do you agree to see a therapist?"

"I can't afford it," I said.

"Our health insurance covers it," he said.

"How do you know?" I asked.

"I checked," he said.

"Oh, so you've been thinking about this for a while." I wanted to set the cup down, but I saw a crumb on the table.

"I want to do what's good for everyone." He stared out into the store.

"I don't know if I can talk to a stranger," I said. "It's too personal."

"You have to do something to help yourself. For your own good." He picked at a spot on his jeans, distracting me.

"I have to think about it." I wiped my face and then realized my hand had touched dirty things. My eye twitched.

Howard studied me. "Go home and let me know what you've decided tomorrow."

"So that's it? Therapy or get fired?" My eyes welled up, but I had learned to control my tears and I also didn't have my hypoallergenic tissues.

"That's it," he said.

I put my head down, grabbed my bag, and ran home. My head spun as I imagined everyone at work discussing my issues as if I was a psych patient. I hated them for it.

AFTER A SHOWER, I waited for my piano teacher to arrive. Mother hired Max to help me with my Juilliard audition. I used to go see him at the Institute for Music but after Mother died, I felt it was best if he came to the house. I always felt sick thinking about touching the public pianos. It thought it would be easier to clean up after one person.

The doorbell rang and I walked down the edge of the stairs so I wouldn't dirty them.

"Hi, Ellen," said Max as I opened the door. He always made it a point to say my name.

"Hi, Max," I reciprocated.

He carefully removed his shoes, tiptoed up the stairs, and washed his hands in the kitchen sink. After all these years, he knew the drill. "Are you ready?"

He stood so close to me; I could smell his minty gum. I stepped back. His hot breath made me feel strange—not dirty, but off-kilter.

"Are you going to try out this year?" he asked.

"I don't know. I'm not sure if I'm ready yet." I had just turned twenty-five, and I'd be competing with child prodigies.

Why was I still paying Max to show up? I couldn't really afford it. I suppose if he disappeared from my life, I'd have to reorder things again. That would be too much work.

"Is there something in particular you want to work on?" he asked.

"What do you think about people who see shrinks?" I asked.

"Shrinks? You mean a psychologist or psychiatrist?" He lowered himself on the covered piano bench.

"Yeah, or a therapist," I said.

"My brother is a psychiatrist. They can prescribe meds." He frowned. "Why do you ask?"

"Just heard people talk about it. It sounds so serious. Are there any alternatives?"

"Have you tried hypnosis?" he asked.

"Where they make you cluck like a chicken?" I asked.

Max laughed. "They can't make you do anything you don't want to do."

"Really? I couldn't be so out of control." I eyed our footprints in the carpet.

"It's like meditation." He closed his eyes and breathed in through his mouth.

"Like Buddhism, I guess." My face flushed again. I had exposed too much of myself.

"Kind of, a lot of self-reflection, breathing, and self-calming. It's nothing to be ashamed of. My brother says it helps if you're open to it." He looked at his watch.

"Oh, sorry, do you have a lesson after this?" I asked.

"Actually, I have a Skype interview. It's for a teaching position at Boston U."

"Boston, Massachusetts? You're leaving?"

"If I get the job, yes."

"You'd move that far from your life?"

"If I moved to Boston, that would be my new life."

"Oh," I said.

"I've been thinking about it for a while. I'm turning thirty next week, and I'm still living with my parents. Going professional never panned out. It's time to grow up."

"You seem like you have it all together," I said.

"Fake it until you make it." He laughed.

"I guess you should go. I'll still pay you for your time."

"It's cool. Do you have a therapist in mind? I can ask my brother for recommendations."

"I don't think I can see a doctor. Can you text me the name of a hypnotist?"

"I'll do it after my interview."

"Okay," I whispered.

"If I get the job, I'll say good-bye before I go." He moved closer to me as if he was going to hug me and I stepped back.

The one person I trusted to see my dysfunction was leaving me. Mother was right not to let anyone into her life. That way no one can hurt you by leaving.

Two hours later, Max texted Shane West's contact information. "Great hypnotist!"

I put my music books in my "M" stack. No more lessons. If I needed them again, I knew where to find them. Next, I vacuumed the carpet to erase Max's memory from the house. If I finished washing the clothes I wore today, I could still get to bed before midnight.

HOWARD WAS WAITING for me at work the next morning. "I thought we could talk before the others showed up."

"Okay." I hoped he had reconsidered his demand.

"Did you think about what we talked about?" he asked.

"I asked around. A hypnotist is as good as a shrink. It'll teach me to relax. I know it can help me." I fixated on the dirt Howard had tracked in.

"Do you have someone in mind?" he asked.

"Shane West," I said. "He's kind of famous. He's been on the radio helping people stop smoking or lose weight."

"Can he help you?" he asked.

"Can I keep my job? I wouldn't know what to do if I couldn't come here. I'd go cra . . ." Mother would have thrown a fit if she heard me use that word. *Crazy. Crazy. Crazy.*

"Are you sure he can help you?" Howard sat down, put his elbows on his knees, and covered his face with his hands.

"Please," I pleaded.

"Go call him." He took more time than normal to straighten out the bottom half of his jeans, pressing down both legs several times. When he caught me staring, he blushed.

"Just be careful what you say to the other employees," he said. "I know how people can judge."

"No one talks to me anyway," I said.

SHANE ASKED ME a few questions on the phone and then emailed a three-page profile questionnaire. I explained to Howard how competent Shane must be if he was recommended by a psychiatrist.

Waiting for the appointment was awful. I kept waking up in the middle of the night to check on the locked doors. During the day, I obsessed about what color dress I had worn to my middle school graduation. I couldn't remember if it was blue or purple, causing me to tear through my photo albums until I had the answer. I wondered if the hypnotist could help me, or if I should see a doctor as Howard requested.

Shane's office was on the first floor of his townhouse. I was already anxious when he informed me that he had cats. But when I arrived, the house was clean and smelled fresh.

"I'm going to record the sessions then send you the audio files so you can listen to them later if you want to. I've read your intake forms. Let's go over a few things so I can understand what you want to accomplish." He scrolled through his iPad.

I continued to stand, staring at his recliner. I wondered

how many people had sat there.

Shane handed me a rag and a bottle of leather cleaner. "Go ahead; clean it if it makes you feel better."

A speck of sweat rolled off my face. "It's okay."

"No, I want you to be comfortable. I'll leave the room and you can do what you need to do." Shane looked at his watch and left.

When he returned, I was still polishing the chair. "Are you ready?"

"Yes, I think I can relax," I said.

"Good, please sit and we'll begin."

I eased back and put my feet up.

"What brought you to me?" he asked.

"My boss asked me to seek treatment," I said.

"For what?" he asked.

"Anxiety. Control issues."

"Do you think you have a problem?" he asked.

"Maybe," I said.

"If you don't acknowledge you have issues to work on, you won't get well."

"I know but I've never . . ." I was about to say I haven't done anything crazy but that's not exactly true.

"What is your idea of a perfect day?" he asked.

"Not worrying," I said.

"What do you worry about?" He leaned back in his chair.

"Germs. Order. Safety."

"Do you think someone will break into your house, kick over your piles of stuff, and touch your pillows with their muddy hands?" I had almost forgotten about the lengthy questionnaires I'd filled out.

I shrugged.

"If everything you imagined came to life, what's the worst thing that could happen to you? Would you die? Would you suffer? Would you lose friends?" He waited for a response. I couldn't think of one thing.

"Close your eyes. Let's do a breathing exercise. You can do this when you feel anxious. Practice every day until I see you next week. Think of a place you want to be. Where is that place?"

"I've always wanted to go to the beach," I said.

"Feel the cool breeze on your face. You're safe. Dip your toe into the sand. Make a ten in the sand with your toe. Then a nine. Eight. Seven. Six. Five. Four. Three. Two. One."

I felt like I was floating.

"You're perfectly safe. If you want, you can still get up and leave. I don't control you. Understand?"

"Yes." I wiggled my toes just to make sure he was telling the truth.

"What are you most afraid of?" he asked.

I felt a jolt down my back. "My mother."

"What's her name?"

"Soon Ae Kim."

"Where is she?"

"In the house."

"She lives with you?"

"No, she's in an urn on top of the piano."

"She's dead?"

"Yes."

"So, how is she disturbing you?" he asked.

"Nothing is clean enough for her," I said.

"Let's come back. You are counting the pebbles on the beach. One. Two. Three. Four. Five. When you open your eyes, you will feel rested. Six. Seven. Eight. Nine. Ten. Open your eyes."

I felt drowsy but relaxed.

"How do you feel?" he asked.

"Why did you bring me out of it?" I asked.

Shane turns off the recording. "Ellen, perhaps I'm not the one to help you. Perhaps you may need more, let's say, advanced help."

"Like a shrink?" I gripped the side of the chair.

"Let's practice the breathing exercises," he said. "If you want to come back here, you are welcome. I'm just saying perhaps you should seek other help as well."

"I don't want to see a shrink," I said.

"Alright, let's start with three sessions. I'll email the first recording to you this afternoon. Listen to it every day until we meet again next week."

WHEN I WENT back for the session, Shane was consoling a sobbing woman when I arrived at his office. When she saw me, she wiped her tears and ran to her car.

"Sorry, we just broke up." Shane looked at the ceiling.

"It's okay," I said.

"Everyone has issues to work on, even me." He closed door.

"Is she okay?" I asked.

"She's moving back to Ecuador. Her student visa expired. If I marry her, she can stay, but I'm not ready for that type of commitment." He sat at his computer. "I'm sorry, that was too personal."

I sat down on the chair, forgetting to wipe it off. He handed the rag to me. "Do you need a minute?"

I nodded.

He returned after a few minutes. "Have you been doing the exercises?"

"Yes. I still feel anxious, but I can put some things out of my mind." My jaw clenched.

"It's a process. Everyone has anxieties. Some people can deal with them better than others. Some people need medication. It's not a judgment. It's a psychological thing." He sat back down.

I leaned back and closed my eyes.

"Let's count back from ten. Let's go to a happy time in your life," he said. "Where are you?"

"My first day of work at Books & Brews," I said.

"Why are you happy?" he asked.

"Howard made me feel like he needed me," I said. "He didn't make any judgments."

"Whenever you feel anxious, go back to this day and other days when you felt good about yourself. Remember that you can make other happy memories."

I couldn't remember any other days and I stopped talking.

"Let's slowly return. Ten . . ."

I open my eyes.

"We have one more session left. Do you want to continue?" asked Shane.

"I'm not sure," I said.

"Keep doing the exercises consistently. I'll email this week's recording to you."

HOWARD SUGGESTED I stay home for a couple of weeks to work on my exercises. He warned me to take it seriously because the others were itching for me to leave. Since this decision seemed to make everyone else happy, I agreed.

Waiting for my third and final session with Shane, I watched him and his girlfriend outside on the grass locked in an embrace. Her lips said, "Okay, okay." She finally left and I walked up to him.

"I'm getting married," he announced, as if last week never happened.

"Congratulations. Is everything okay now?"

"Everyone has stuff to work out." He chuckled.

"IS THERE SOMETHING you'd like to work on today?" he asked.

"I just want to be like everyone else," I said.

"Be the best person you can be. Remember, what's the worst that can happen if you failed?"

I couldn't think of a single thing.

"Try getting rid of some things you don't need, little by little. Free yourself. You said you might want to travel. Sell some stuff and make some new memories."

I realized I didn't clean the chair. I made it through the session without thinking about it. I felt dirty, but I could wash my clothes when I got home.

"Listen to the recordings for twenty-one days. Do the self-hypnosis every night. After a while, it will feel natural."

"Will I get better?" I asked.

"Better is a relative term. If you need to speak to me, please don't hesitate to call. It's not bad to ask for help. It doesn't make you weak."

IN THE TWO months since my consultation with Shane, I'd made progress by shredding my stacks up to "D". There were setbacks. Howard threatened to fire me at least ten times. Everyone at Books & Brews still ignored me. The customers still waited for other workers to serve them.

I read about a music therapy class at a halfway house, I donated the piano to them. When the movers took it away, I felt as if every day of the last twenty years were tearing away my skin. I slept in the indented spot in the carpet for days.

I told Howard I needed to take my Mother's ashes to the ocean. He gave me a week's paid leave to reward me for my progress. He said if I needed more time, I could take it.

I set the urn in the sand next to me. I suppose she'd hoped I'd keep her ashes. But I had to free us both. She never escaped her fears in life. Maybe she didn't want to hurt me. Maybe I'll never know what she went through. Maybe I can be okay with not knowing.

I waded into the warm water, squeezed the sand between my toes, and emptied the urn.

Lazy Sundays

*D*ear *Atlanta Police Department:*

I'm leaving my diary and a set of photos with Anne Jamison. If you're reading this, something has happened to me. Copies have also been sent to certain media outlets in case your officers have been paid off by my husband.

I've gone back and added background information about each incident when appropriate.

Sincerely,
Natasha Leach

May 1
He only beats me on Sunday afternoons. He knows the bruises will heal by the next week, when he goes to church and worships his God. He calls it our lazy Sundays. After his preaching, after all my charitable activities, alone, just the two of us, we practice our ritual.

I met Samuel in Bible study at Southern Heaven Sanctuary. I was in awe of him for the first few months. He knew so much about scripture, reciting all the books from the New Testament from memory. I couldn't believe how lucky I was to have found such a righteous man.

The first time he hit me, the stinging in my mouth spread to my heart and squeezed it. I looked down. Fresh blood splattered on top of crusted dark spots on his worn carpet. Together they made swirling patterns that rivaled modern art. I bit my bottom lip to stop myself from crying. I knew he was a good man. I knew he wouldn't have hit me if I hadn't somehow provoked him.

"I need you to help me get closer to God." He shivered in my arms. "It won't happen again. It won't happen again."

I prayed for him then. I pray for him still. I pray he won't hit me again. I pray no one will find out. I sit in my pew and no one knows why I weep, heaving silently. I've prayed for the last fourteen years.

He hits me again. And again. It doesn't seem to matter if it is after dinner with friends or after dressing down a store clerk. He always seems to be relieved afterwards. "I have all this energy to serve God," he says as he embraces my broken body.

Every Sunday, I debate whether or not I should attend to my responsibilities: overseas building missions, the women's prayer group, counseling sessions.

I always decide it is too embarrassing to disappear while everyone else is working so hard. What would my excuse be for leaving? Would it be worth the beating? I know I would be punished either way.

It was harder in the beginning. I worked full-time and had not learned to cover up the bruises so masterfully. The first few times, he tore flesh and knocked out teeth. He learned to hold back a bit. He began to hit me in the stomach and back, where no one would see the bruises. We both learned to mask our secret. In time, we mastered our craft.

"You should quit your job," he said, six months into our marriage.

"They need me there," I said.

"I need to know where you are at all times. I love you that much." He smiled.

"I need to give sufficient notice. I've been there for three years." He looked at me and I knew it was the end of our discussion.

May 15

For our first anniversary, he made a plaque and hung it over our garage door. He pointed at it whenever we passed it:

Wives, submit to your own husbands, as to the Lord. For the husband is the head of the wife even as Christ is the head of the church, his body, and is himself its Savior. Now as the church submits to Christ, so also wives should submit in everything to their husbands.
—Ephesians 5:22-33

I didn't dare tell him he omitted the rest of the passage. It wasn't worth it.

Husbands, love your wives, just as Christ loved the church and gave himself up for her to make her holy, cleansing her by the washing with water through the word, and to present her to himself as a radiant church, without stain or wrinkle or any other blemish, but holy and blameless. In this same way, husbands ought to love their wives as their own bodies. He who loves his wife loves himself.

May 23
Samuel's secretary started following me immediately after my wedding. She spends the entire Sunday sitting in her car, spying on me with her pink binoculars. She takes photos on her phone and sends them to Samuel. She records furiously in her notebook.

During the week, she ignores me. I make it into the offices usually on Wednesdays or Thursdays, after I can walk again. Elise doesn't make eye contact with me. She leaves the office when I enter.

May 31
I'm thankful for Samuel's time at the studio. It's at least two hours away from me.

Shortly after taking over the ministry, he started broadcasting on a local cable access show. Ten years later, the church has its own studio which sends daily messages to more than thirty thousand subscribers.

He loves his stardom. What would his fans think if they found out what he does in private?

September 3

Over the years, the famous and the infamous have come to Samuel for guidance. What a joke. If they only knew what a monster he really was.

November 6

Anne Jamison from Second Chances Halfway House reached out to the women's ministry last year. I'm thankful for the time with her and away from Samuel.

Her halfway house had gained attention after it was featured on ABC News with Diane Sawyer, naming her Person of the Week. She suggested in her meeting with Samuel that I sit on the Board of Directors. Anything that boosted his visibility excited him, so he agreed.

On Sundays after church, I would drive down to counsel the women. Anne noticed my achiness right away. "Your dead eyes were a clue," she said. I suppose she recognized a certain desperation in me, something she saw in herself.

"You can stay here," she said.

"I don't know what you're talking about."

"I understand what you're going through." She touches my shoulder.

"I'm supposed to be helping the women here, not living here. It's too embarrassing."

"Dead is worse than embarrassed," she said.

December 13

Anne gave me a Taser gun. She asked if I knew how to use it. I told her I couldn't take it. She insisted. She has been a real friend to me. She is the only person I trust.

February 9

When I met Samuel, he told me he was an orphan. I told a friend at church how my heart went out to him. She told me he was the son of our church's pastor. I confronted him and he immediately fell into my arms.

"My mother left when I was eight years old. My bitch of a stepmother sent me to boarding school. My father let her do it. That's the same as being an orphan." I accepted his lie and felt sorrier for him because he had to create a coping mechanism to forget his childhood.

He was like a child at first. He wrapped his arms around my waist while he laid his head in my lap. I couldn't go anywhere without him looking for me. He wanted me to cook for him every night. He wanted a mother—he wanted his mother, who fled like a monster.

I'm grateful I can't have children. I was pregnant once, early in our marriage. Samuel was out with Yogi and their female fans. I was angry when he got home. Why did I choose to have a backbone that night? I've asked myself that every day for twelve years. He was drunk, possibly high. I threatened to leave.

"Nobody leaves me," he yelled. He kicked my stomach, knowing I was in my second trimester. I felt wetness run down my legs. He was used to seeing my blood flow and kept slapping me. He didn't realize what he'd done until I howled like an animal.

I should have pressed charges then, but he begged me not to. "You will crush the church. Think of all the parishioners who would be lost."

The police questioned me at the hospital. The one in charge was a deacon at our church. I heard Samuel tell him I slipped in the tub.

"I'm so sorry, Pastor," said the officer as he wiped away a tear.

"Sorry, ma'am."

I never got pregnant again. And I'm grateful.

June 21

Ginny Lard, one of the halfway house residents, bumped into me today. "Oh, sorry," she said.

I smiled. I'm not sure if she remembered where she met me before. Her husband's memorial service was at our church. A handful of strippers, drunkards, and gang members showed up. Ginny, the dutiful wife, sat in the front row, alone. No other family members attended.

Samuel gave a heartfelt sermon, crying as much as the strippers did. Many appeared to have come straight from their job.

"Isn't it great to save lost souls?" he asked his secretary. She stood against the wall, pressing herself as flat as she could, as Freddie's friends filed out.

The club had been shut down. Freddie was found in his office, stabbed forty-two times. The police found Ginny drunk at the bar. She was arrested, but the police couldn't find her fingerprints on the knife.

Most wives around town would say Freddie's murder was justified. If their husbands were ever missing, they were either dead or having a bender at the club.

Freddie had been busted several times for drugs, prostitution, and child pornography. Somehow, he always escaped the charges.

June 29

I know he'll kill me someday and I need to make sure there's proof that he did it. At first, I asked for God's strength. I asked him to give Samuel guidance, to free both of us. I've come to realize God won't help me.

Anne told me to take photos of my abuse. Each one is labeled with the date.

July 6

I want him to love me as much as I love him. The doctor asked me what happened to me. Samuel's father, Pastor Timothy, asked me not to say anything. He said Samuel is going to be a great leader. If I turn him in, I'll be ruining the lives of people he could have helped.

How can I argue with that? Mama said it's the wife's duty to stand by her man, no matter what. She said the black eye will heal. Where would I find another good man from a good, upstanding family? No one else would take me after they find out what trailer park we rolled out of. She says he's better than my father ever was. She says these people, the Leaches, are angels. She doesn't know about our lazy Sundays. But I don't think she'd care if she did.

July 9

I'm not allowed to talk to Mama anymore even though she takes his side. Samuel said people are clouding my judgment.

July 16

I went to Pastor Timothy for help again. He said Samuel would calm down with age. "God rewards those who are patient," he said.

August 17

I lost a tooth. A dentist friend of Pastor Timothy gave me an implant. He's quite old. He looks at me with pity. He tells me he's worked on several generations of Leach women.

September 9

I lost it at church today. I wept so loudly, Samuel gave me the evil eye.

After the service, he stomped on my foot and broke my toe.

He still made me wear heels around the house the next day. He warned me about flinching during his sermons.

October 23

I had to throw out a blouse today. Samuel jumped me in the garage. He couldn't wait for our lazy Sunday. I don't know how much more I can take.

December 26

Swollen eye. Sprained wrist. Nothing broken this time. Can't write anymore today.

February 9

He cut me today with a whip. I didn't think anything could hurt more than his hands. These scars probably won't go away.

They didn't. Anne has the photos.

May 23

He tells me the women at Freddie's club are prettier than I am. I'm lucky someone married me. I should be grateful to him.

April 30

I feel like I'm dead already.

August 29

Samuel is becoming more depraved. He's going to kill me soon. I may welcome it.

January 17

Last night Samuel came home, smelling like liquor and cheap perfume. He jumped on top of me and put his hand over my nose.

"You're all whores!" He went on autopilot, clamping his hand tighter around my face.

I coughed, gasping for air.

"What do you pray for?" he kept asking.

Seven hundred and twenty-eight times. Every blow he handed me rushed through my mind. I looked into his eyes. I knew he would kill me if I fought him.

"Get me a drink," he said.

I nodded, his hand still over my face. He let me up and he fell on the bed. When I returned from the kitchen, he was passed out. I kicked him. I rolled him over to his side. He moaned but didn't wake up.

I wanted to kill him but I didn't have it in me. I ripped the keys off his neck and opened the safe where his financial statements were kept. I shoved them into my purse and left him a note.

Dear Samuel,

You have donated all your Earthly possessions to charities close to my heart. A press release will be sent out letting the world know what a great man you are. Don't try to find me. If you attempt to get back a cent of the money, I will release your real financial statements.

There won't be any more lazy Sundays for us. Sunday, and every other day, will be for me from now on.

Natasha

Reunion

He was my first friend at Liberty Elementary. Our third-grade teacher had seated us alphabetically, Killian then Lemmen. The blonde boy turned and looked at me without saying a word. I looked down at my gingham dress from Goodwill. I was embarrassed because all the other kids wore brand-name clothes.

"Psst. Hey, my name is Matt."

"Hi," I whispered.

"Hey, you got a name?"

"Wynter."

"Winter, like spring, summer, and fall?" he asked. He leaned back so his head was on my desk and looked upwards into my face.

I rocked in my seat. "No, it's spelled with a 'Y'".

"Okay, Wynter what?" Matt grinned and it eased my nerves.

"Lemmen." I waited for a shiver because of my first name or a puckering noise because of my last name. He didn't comment on either.

"Okay, I'll talk to you at recess." Matt's smile confused me. No one had ever accepted me without question before.

It was always easy with him. I didn't have to explain that my mother didn't want me. She wished for a baby boy born in the sunlight, not a girl entering the world under the cold, winter moon. When the nurse asked for a name, I imagine my mother must have looked at the fogged-up window in her hospital room and said, "Winter."

Without a husband or family member there to stop her, the nurse wrote down the name and left. I often imagine the nurse taking pity on me and changing the spelling to somehow soften its meaning.

My mother was an only child of parents who didn't approve of my father. She had chosen a man over her family and was promptly disowned. Within months of their marriage, my father chose a seventeen-year-old girl over my mother. My mother's love dried up, cracking the umbilical cord that normally bonded mother and child.

I realized Matt recognized a certain sadness in me—something others could not put a finger on but was as familiar to him as his own skin. He never asked about my parents like the others did. It didn't seem to matter to him.

Once, during recess as he pushed me on the swing, Matt told me his mother was away at a special resort. No one could talk to her for ninety days.

"Or more . . ." His voice trailed off as he pushed me higher and higher on the swing, and further and further away from our reality. We didn't speak of our absent parents again.

"When we leave this town, we can be everything we want to be," he said, but the deadness in his eyes said otherwise.

"I don't understand why people can't leave me alone," I told him.

"If they think it doesn't bother you, they'll stop."

As we drifted into different cliques over the years, we spoke less. Always kind but distant, he nodded his head when he saw me, as if to say, "I understand."

Near the end of our senior year, I sheepishly asked who he was taking to prom. I was interrupted by cackling.

"He's taking me, wide-load," said Hannah, the head cheerleader. "Who else would the quarterback take to prom?"

Matt looked at me as if he wanted to apologize for her. He then crossed his eyes to make her laugh. He danced around and everyone in the hallway jumped in. Grabbing Hannah around the shoulders, he led her away. He turned and winked at me, saving me again.

When the prom king and queen nominations were announced, I urged my science club members to cast their votes for Matt.

"Why do you care if that arrogant ass wears the crown?" asked Curtis, my lab partner.

"He's my friend," I said.

"No, he's not. Friends are who you hang out with. He doesn't even acknowledge that you're alive. We're more your friends than he is, and we don't even know where you live." Curtis threw up his hands in disgust. "After graduation, you'll never see him again."

"But you'll still vote for him, right?" I know I sounded foolish, but I imagined Matt asking me to dance when he found out I made everyone vote for him. But in the end, I didn't go to the prom. I never got that dance.

AFTER GRADUATION, MATT came to my house. It didn't seem real. He had never visited me before.

"You know where I live?"

"Let's have lunch. Come on, I'll drive."

He didn't speak until our food arrived. "My father says my mother is dead."

"When did she die?" He hadn't said anything about her since third grade.

"It doesn't matter. She's not coming back." Matt took a bite of his greasy cheeseburger.

I nodded my head. Our unspoken rule was not to push each other too far into reality.

"We had her cremated. Pastor Leach said what she did was a sin. He wouldn't perform the ceremony. Fucking hypocrite."

"I'm sorry," I said. The kids called Pastor Leach *Pastor Letch* behind his back. I had heard he'd slept with several women in the church and some of the football players said they'd seen him hanging out with undesirables in the alleyways of

Atlanta. Of course, the football players were out using their fake IDs during these observations, so the talk had been in very low tones.

"Let's leave town," I told Matt.

"I'm supposed to be the fourth generation to run the body shop. I have to stay. I have to carry on the legacy."

We both knew *legacy* meant more than the business. He briefly held my hand, for once not worrying what others thought. Then he pulled away.

"I have to leave," I told him. "My mother is getting worse. I'm not like you, Matt. I don't have the patience for it."

"Do what makes you happy."

"You've never mentioned happiness before—yours or mine," I said.

"Good luck," said Matt.

"See you at the tenth reunion," I said.

"We should be fixed up by then." He gave me his trademark nod.

I smiled, hoping that happiness was out there for both of us.

WALKING FIVE BLOCKS to the funeral home from the hotel, I braced myself for a room full of Matt's high school friends. When I entered the viewing room, only a handful of people were present.

"Ms. Lemmen, I'm sorry for your loss. I hope we've done everything to your satisfaction. With you not being here to make the selections, we could only guess what you wanted." Mr. Blanton, the funeral director, looked down at the carpet, his hands straight down at his sides.

"I'm sure you've made all the right decisions. Please don't tell anyone that I paid for the funeral." I looked over my shoulder and was relieved no one had overheard us.

"Of course, Ms. Lemmen. May I show you inside?"

"No, I'll find my way. Thank you, Mr. Blanton." I left him

and made my way into the back row of seats.

"Did you know him well?" asked a woman with a familiar voice.

"He was my best friend," I told her.

"Who are you again?" Her sharp tone dug into my sadness.

I recognized her now. Same Hannah but older.

"I heard he torched the garage. My husband disagrees and says Matt's father fell asleep with a cigarette in his mouth again. It happened a few times before, but Matt had always been able to put out the fire. You know, they lived above the garage. Matt wouldn't leave him." She leaned in to continue her gossip.

"I don't care about that," I said.

"What a shame. He had so much promise. Never married. No kids. Lived with his alcoholic father. Never would have gone to prom with him if I'd known what a loser he'd become."

I waved her off. As I rose from the pew, I dug my heel into Hannah's foot and twisted it.

"Bitch!" screamed Hannah. People turned and looked, making her hunch down in her seat.

Breathing deeply, I braced myself to say goodbye to my old friend. I looked at the boy who had accepted me—overweight, buck-toothed, bumpy nose, and all. My liposuction, narrowed nose, and veneers wouldn't have impressed him at all.

As he rested in his coffin, I recognized a peace in him—a peace we searched for all our lives, a peace I thought was unattainable. He taught me a final lesson. I knew time would smooth over the jagged edges of my heart and life would hurt a little less.

"It's not all bad," Matt had always told me.

Perhaps he was right.

Perhaps there was some happiness in my life.

Perhaps it was time to accept myself, as Matt had accepted me.

"We'll have our reunion someday, in a better place." I kissed him for the first and last time.

Letting Go

The early risers and loyal customers have tracked in mud, crumbled leaves, and the last of summer's ailing bugs into Books & Brews, my coffee shop and bookstore. The sight of the mess makes my hands twitch. I hide them in my jeans pockets. My mother always said I was a sensitive soul. My father called it other things.

I tell my assistant manager that I need to take a walk. It clears my head, calms my nerves, and makes me forget the petty things that worry me throughout the day. This is the only habit I've taken from the therapist my mother forced our family to see when I was fifteen.

Dr. Patrick West had suggested I go to ERP—short for Exposure Response Therapy. It's the process of exposing ourselves to our worst fears instead of trying to manage them. He said I showed obsessive compulsive tendencies. He felt my brother's death had made it worse, and said I needed intensive treatment.

"Anxiety doesn't go away, but it can be managed," Dr. West explained. "But we must first identify what is bothering us."

Mother leaned in. The desperation in her eyes scared me.

"Unwanted thoughts are normal, but some people have more unwanted thoughts than others, and those thoughts can become obsessive."

As my father folded his arms, Dr. West raised his eyebrows and pointed his explanation toward my mother.

"This is going to cost a fortune." My father's face turned beet red. "The funeral drained us."

My mother looked at the floor.

"Be a man, and suck it up," my father yelled at me.

"Walter!" My mother blushed.

"Mr. Frank, that's not helpful," said Dr. West. "What's the worst thing that could happen if your son tried ERP?"

My father stood. "No head-shrinker is going to tell me how to raise my kid."

"You need to let your anger go," said Dr. West.

"We're letting *you* go," said my father as he slammed the door behind him.

I was relieved. What would ERP have meant for me? It's supposed to expose your fears by immersing you in your greatest nightmares. I could never let anyone find out what mine were.

MOST DAYS, I think my life is in order. But one morning, Cliff strolls into the coffee shop with his kids. I haven't seen him since the investigation. Before he sees me, I run to the back room.

Cliff's son is around the age my brother Hank was when he died. His daughter is slightly older. They order their hot chocolates and lattes, and leave.

Just like that.

He couldn't have known it was my place. He wouldn't have come. Would he?

Seeing him leads me back into that dark hole. I think I see Hank—at the grocery store, at the bank, everywhere. I visit the park every day, waiting for him to tell me it was all a horrible dream. I sit on the swings where Hank and I sat before they showed up.

"FAG," YELLED TEDDY, the boy from my gym class.

"Let's go, Hank," I whispered in my brother's ear.

"Why?"

"Where are you going, sweetie?" Teddy mocked.

"Run!" I pulled Hank behind me.

Teddy's buddies from the football team circled us.

"Let my brother go," I said.

"Let the kid go," said Teddy's best friend, Cliff.

"Nah, let the kid see what happens to fags," said Teddy. He pushed me into Hank. "Does it run in the family?"

Hank slipped around me and kicked Teddy. Cliff closed his eyes. He seemed to know what was coming. Hank and I didn't.

I think Hank yelled, "Let me go." I have been trying to squash the rest of the memory for thirty years.

The police came to the house a few weeks after the investigation was closed. There wasn't a trial. All the parents, including mine, wanted the situation to go away.

"We're sorry for your loss," the policemen told my parents. They handed Hank's skateboard to my mother. He dragged that thing everywhere he went. The skateboard was worn down in the middle, blood splattered on it. My mother stroked the brownish specks as if she could erase the tragedy. Then she hugged it as if it was Hank, knowing it was the last thing he touched.

"He didn't suffer," one of them told us. This seemed to momentarily ease my mother's mind. She smiled. A proper southern lady, she thanked them for this information.

Only I knew what really happened. After the crowd ran away, I consoled Hank until the ambulance came. My arms still burn with the memory of holding him, his soul leaving his ten-year old body. His didn't die instantly like the police told my parents. He looked at me, as if asking why this had happened to him.

"Why did they do it?" my father asked the policemen.

"Bullying gone wrong," they said.

I never told anyone that Hank's death was my fault. The boys didn't say anything either. This was years before people talked about hate crimes.

They all took plea bargains. Teddy received a year in juvenile detention and two years of probation. The other boys each received six months of probation. Cliff ran home and told his mother what happened. She called the ambulance. For that good deed, he didn't receive one day of punishment.

MY FATHER'S PUCKERED lips, deep sighing, and disappointed looks were the only conversation between us at the dinner table and later at our mandatory holiday meetings. We never spoke of Hank, his life or death. My complicity was clear to everyone, but no one dared to accuse me out loud. We rotted from the inside out.

My father drank as if to fill the void inside him. He died of liver failure about ten years ago. My mother seemed relieved when he passed, but she followed close behind. While cleaning out their house, I found the skateboard tucked away behind Grandma Frank's silver. I trucked it all to a storage facility near my store to be locked away.

I RUN TO the park again. I see a skateboard like Hank used to own. The sight sucker-punches. The board had the same stickers on it, rubbed down and worn.

I wait for some forgetful kid to come back to retrieve it. Day after day, I wait.

I go to the storage unit that houses my mother's prized possessions. I throw everything outside. It's not there. The skateboard and my guilt have escaped into the universe, traveling back to the place where my brother died because I was gay.

I go back to the park again. The strange sensation that I only feel in the darkest hours of the night intensifies. My brain shuts off for a few seconds. A dull *ting* echoes in my head as if a small rubber band is being pulled. *Ting. Ting.*

I pick up the skateboard. A boy, about ten years old, appears out of nowhere. He stares at me.

I push the board out to him.

He stretches out his arms to receive it.

I let it go.

Restitution

The clawing intensifies. It sounds like a lion, muddied feet, trampling across a linoleum floor. The nails scratch everything they touch, swirling dirt and hurt in endless circles.

I haven't slept well since Nathan announced he's running for Congress. He's a cop, a detective on the Atlanta police force. Fed up with what he said the liberals are doing to this country, he declared he would force a change. His waspy family rejoiced.

At the same dinner, he proposed to me. Betsy, his rancid mother, reluctantly parted with his grandmother's ring. "This is an heirloom. We'd want it back if the marriage ever ended." She plastered on her famous Betsy grin. I thought I saw a snake's tongue dangle out of her mouth.

"Mother, please," said Nathan.

"Ashley dear, a Congressman needs a good wife by his side. We'll have the wedding right before the election. It will be headline news. Of course, we'll pay for everything. We know you don't have family." Betsy finished her lecture and left us.

She didn't know I did have money once. When I was orphaned, a trust fund was provided for me, but I was told on my eighteenth birthday that nothing was left. That night, my dead mother sat on my bed and told me to kill my aunt for stealing from me. Of course, I couldn't bring myself to do it, but I did take my aunt's jewelry box. I figured I paid for all the jewelry in it anyway. That's how I funded my first year at Agnes Scott College.

KATHY VAUGHN WAS my roommate. If it wasn't for her, I would have starved that first term. She worked at the college's cafeteria and brought back leftovers for both of us.

Everyone had to leave campus during breaks since all services were closed. Kathy invited me to spend our first winter break with her in Columbus, Georgia. It was about two hours south of campus. Her family lived in a small, ranch style house in an older neighborhood.

That's where I met her brother, Tommy. He invited us to go bowling. Kathy kept throwing out excuses not to go but he wouldn't give up.

He came back to our lane with Cokes and nachos.

"Where do you go to school?" I asked him.

"Kathy's the only smart one in the family. I'm working at the deli on Main Street." He knocked his head with his knuckles.

"Is that all you want to do?" I asked.

"What else is there? Everyone in the family is helping Kathy get through school."

"I wish somebody would help me," I said without realizing I spoke aloud.

"Sorry, I didn't mean to hurt your feelings." Tommy fell silent again.

"It's okay. I'll find a way."

Kathy stood in front of us with her arms crossed. "You going to bowl or not?"

I threw my ball and it rolled into the gutter. Tommy gave me a high five and laughed. Kathy gave him a death stare. Tommy threw a strike. I hugged him. This time, Kathy gave me the look.

The first week into the winter semester, Tommy arrived at our dorm. "Hey sis," he said.

"You can't sleep here," warned Kathy.

"I know, I just came to see you," he said. He looked down and smiled.

"Me? Right. You can come in, but you have to leave before eleven. I'm not getting thrown out because of your infatuation." She glared at me.

"I didn't know he was coming," I said.

"I have to go to work," she said. "Behave yourselves."

We didn't. At first, Tommy came up on weekends. I managed to get a job off-campus for the spring term. Tommy suggested that the three of us get an apartment together near the college.

"No, I'm going to be an RA next year," said Kathy. "It pays room and board, so I won't need extra money from the family."

"What? I didn't know you applied for the job. What am I going to do? I don't want to move to a run-down apartment way off campus. I don't know if I can stay here without a roommate," I said. I didn't mean Tommy should support me, but my needs became greater as my sophomore year progressed. Tuition, lab fees, tutoring, field trips. Tommy already had a job at some strip club in Atlanta to keep me in school.

SUMMER CAME AGAIN and I suggested I wait tables at the club. Two part-time jobs and going to school wasn't working. I was still short three thousand dollars for the fall semester. I knew I could make that in two months serving drinks at the club.

"No, I won't let you do that," said Tommy.

"What do you mean you won't let me?" I asked.

"You don't know what goes on there. The owner is screwing all the girls. They're all on drugs. They'll talk you into stripping. It always happens to the waitresses." Tommy leaned back into the couch and covered his face with his hands.

"I can't keep going on like this." I slid down on the floor next to the couch. "I'm going to have to drop out."

"I'll get you the money. You won't have to work at all next semester."

"From where?"

"Don't worry. I'll always take care of you." Tommy held me and I thought I could love him forever.

Tommy delivered the tuition money to me a few days before

it was due. The cash was in a plastic bag, as if he'd found it on the side of the street.

"Where did you get this?" I asked.

"Just a side job from the club," he said. He went straight to the bathroom.

"Thanks, babe," I said as he closed the door. As I stacked the bills on the table, I realized it was enough for junior and senior year. At the time, I didn't care how he'd managed to get it. I just wanted to finish school.

"What did you say?" he asked from the bathroom.

I ran into the bathroom and hugged him. "You came through for me. No one has ever been on my side since my parents died."

Tommy looked up at the mirror. He had a bruised eye and swollen lip. "I got you, Ash."

I grabbed and kissed him.

"Ouch."

"I'm sorry."

"You need to convert that into a money order before you go to the registration office."

"Why?"

"It just looks suspicious, is all. Don't tell Kathy about this." He closed his eyes.

"Is it illegal?"

"Just looks like it might be. It's okay. I have to get back to work."

Tommy was out later and more often, picking up odd jobs from the club's owner. He worked all night and slept all day. During the spring semester of my junior year, Tommy was arrested. He said his co-workers would bail him out. He wouldn't let me use the tuition money.

"You can't bring that crinkled up stack of bills to court," he said.

Tommy and his gang were convicted of armed robbery. I sat in the back of the courtroom as they led him away. Since he made me promise to stay home, I slouched down so he wouldn't see me.

On the way out of the courtroom, Kathy grabbed my arm. "Did you know Tommy joined a gang?"

"No, I had no idea." I let her dig her nails into my arm.

"You live with him, but you didn't know he robbed six gas stations? You're either clueless or a liar." She pushed me away.

"I go to school all day and he works at night. We hardly see each other." I hoped she didn't see the panic in my eyes.

"You did this to him. It's your fault," she said.

"I swear, I didn't know." I touched her arm. She swung around and slapped me.

"Stay away from him or you'll pay."

"I swear I didn't know," I yelled as she stormed out of the courtroom.

I WAKE UP in a cold sweat. Nathan is at the foot of the bed staring at me. I'm afraid he has heard my fears. He's been spending more nights at his house since my tossing and turning has gotten worse. He tells me I've been screaming, but he doesn't elaborate on the details.

"Are you okay?" he asks.

I nod my head, wiping away the sweat dripping from my hair. It's soaked, as if I took a lap in the pool. But the moisture isn't cool; it's an oil slick.

"Have you thought about quitting your job?" he asks.

"You know how hard I've worked to get this far."

"Why don't you work at one of the family's trusts. All the Smith wives do."

I scroll through my phone to stop the lecturing.

"I need you to start traveling with me," he says. "My mother says you have to be seen on the campaign trail."

"Yes, or else Betsy will have my head. Or at the very least, my ring finger," I say.

"I'm giving a speech at your alma mater on Sunday," says Nathan.

"Agnes Scott?" I haven't been back there since I graduated. I wipe my sweaty palms on my pajamas.

"I need you to come with me."

"How can I help you by going there?" I ask, pulling the covers over my head.

"You're a success story. We need to show these young women that you're one of them, and that you support our goals."

"Well, don't mention that rape law. The campus has always been liberal. You're not going to win any female votes that way." I don't agree with his platform, but I want to help him win.

Nathan flips the channel from CNN to his conservative talk show. "I'm glad you'll be there to support my cause. Don't you agree abortion is a sin even if it's from rape?"

"Do you really believe that?" I ask.

"It doesn't matter. It's the party line. If I don't push this law, I'll lose the support of the hard-liners." Nathan takes my hand. "Will you help me?"

"I have to get changed. We're having a baby shower at work today. I'll see you at Betsy's tonight." I rummage through the closet to find the least offensive outfit so I don't set off my future mother-in-law, again.

"Abortion is a sin," I repeat, until it almost sounds natural. "Abortion is a sin."

MY MARKETING ASSISTANT informed me three weeks ago she would be leaving after the baby shower. Four years of Duke University and five years of hard work at a commercial brokerage firm will be thrown away so she can be a full-time mother. I suppose rich girls don't fully appreciate what it costs some of us, financially and emotionally, to finish school.

I lug the baby seat I bought for her into the break room. There, I see the baby again. It's appeared in many forms and many places over the years. The emaciated baby sits on the counter and watches me from across the room. Its bugged-out eyes follow me. It seems as though it knows me.

The receptionist comes in with the cake and diverts my attention away from the baby. I turn back and the ugly thing is gone. During the party, I feel as if something is watching me through the glass doors.

NATHAN'S CAMPAIGN MANAGER thinks it would be more effective if the speech is in my old dorm's lobby. It is round and grand. Two winding staircases lead up to the second floor where Southern beauties once stood and waited for their gentlemen callers to arrive.

At Betsy's request, I practice controlling my facial expressions. "Eye rolling is forbidden," she warns. I promised her I would try.

Nathan toes the party line—kill universal healthcare, kill gun laws, kill federal interference with state laws, kill convicts, kill public assistance to welfare recipients, but don't kill unborn babies.

Betsy watches my every twitch then nags them out of me. Her son will be President of the United States one day and an orphaned trash box won't get in the way of her plans. I'm distracted by someone who looks familiar. I look away from Nathan. Betsy digs her nails into my arm and whispers in my ear, "Get it together. You won't ruin this for Nathan."

"I thought I saw someone I knew," I try to explain.

"I don't care if you saw your dead mother. You just sit there and smile like a good wife." A small speck of blood dots my sleeve.

"I'm sorry. I lost myself." I try to cover up the red stain. I look inside the grand hall and glance up the stairs. Kathy is there, holding a baby. I look away, holding myself together until Nathan's speech is over. I leave without saying good-bye.

I REMEMBER SITTING for hours on that staircase after I visited Tommy in prison. I can still see his face when I told him I was dating a frat boy. "You said you would wait," he said. "I'm in here for you."

"I'm sorry." I tried to grab his hands but the guard came over to stop me. During the struggle, I caught a glimpse of Tommy's mutilation.

"No," cried Tommy as he pulled his hand away.

"What happened?" I put my hand over my mouth.

"Nothing, there was an accident." The color drained from his face.

"I'm sorry." A sharp pain shot from my abdomen to my own fingers. I pressed down on my stomach.

"Are you pregnant?" he asked. "Kathy said you've been sick."

"No," I said. I couldn't say I wasn't pregnant anymore. He was Catholic. He wouldn't have understood.

He grabbed me. "Did you get an abortion?"

"Don't be ridiculous," I said, pushing him off.

"Tell me you didn't do it."

"I have to leave now," I said.

"I'm sorry I couldn't be what you wanted me to be," he said.

"I'm sorry," I said, as I ran from the room.

"All I wanted was to make you happy," he yelled after me.

I never saw him again.

A YEAR LATER, I was admiring my cap and gown as I stood in front of the full-length mirror in my room at the sorority house. Kathy threw open my bedroom door and lunged at me. "He's dead, you bitch! You killed him."

My cap flew off my head. I peeled her fingers from my

throat. I coughed, trying to catch my breath.

"Tommy's dead!" she wailed. "He killed himself because he couldn't live without you. A slut like you. Someone who killed his child."

I stood there, unable to defend myself. I caused this. "What do you want me to do?"

"I want you to suffer a long, miserable life. I want you to feel Tommy's pain and desperation. I want to watch it happen."

"I didn't want him to die," I said.

Trembling, I backed into the wall.

"You'll see me again," she said.

The sorority sisters rushed me to the hospital. The doctor gave me a sedative. I missed my graduation.

THE MORNING OF my wedding, Kathy ambushes me in the pastor's office where I'm getting ready.

"Why are you here?" I ask.

"You look like you've seen a ghost." She lifts my veil.

"What do you want?" I stand still, hoping she will vanish like she has the many other times she's come to punish me.

"Your soon-to-be husband can't win the congressional seat. We need information on him so we can stop him."

"You expect me to help you?" I ask.

"Yes, or I will be forced to tell your new family about the armed robbery, the abortion, the suicide. Dirty little secrets never go away." She smiles.

"Would you expose Tommy like that?" I ask.

"He's dead. No one can hurt him now, not even you."

I look at my Valentino dress in the mirror. It doesn't make me as beautiful as I thought it would. My sunken eyes still overshadow the couture gown.

"He won't stop. His mother won't let him."

"There are rumors about his protests during his college days. You knew him then. You know the friends he hung out with. We need names."

"What for?" A tingling chill trickles up my spine.

"There was a bombing at an abortion clinic. Perhaps it's the one where you killed Tommy's baby."

"You'll never prove it," I tell her.

"We don't have to. A small rumor is all it takes these days."

"Then why do you need me?" I ask.

"In case we need you to verify the story."

"Me? I wasn't there."

Kathy laughs and throws a file at me. "Then you'll lie."

The file hits the bottom of my dress and sends up a puff of dust. "What's this?"

"Your intake papers from the abortion clinic," she says.

"These are supposed to be confidential," I whisper.

"For such a manipulator, you're naïve. Anything can be bought."

"You may stop the wedding, but you can't stop them."

"Either way, you're going down. I promised Tommy you would never be happy."

"Nathan is a good man. He's not evil like the rest of them."

"He's the enemy. He would do the same if he had the chance."

A tap at the door stops my heart. "Mrs. Smith says it's time," says Betsy's assistant.

"I don't want to delay the wedding of the century." Kathy rips the file from my hands. "You might want to dust yourself off."

"Wait," I say.

"I'll visit you at your house next time." Kathy winks at me and walks out the side door.

"Who was that?" asks the confused girl.

"Someone I used to know," I say.

"Everybody is waiting for you," she says.

I DON'T REMEMBER the ceremony. Nathan is at my side when I wake up in the hospital.

"Where am I?" I notice bars on the windows.

"The doctor says you should stay here for a while." He looks at his watch.

"How long?" I ask.

"We'll decide that in a few days. We just want you to get well." He looks at his text messages.

"I'm fine," I say.

"Are you seeing things again?" He doesn't look at me.

"Yes." I look at the door that is locked from the outside. The bolt clicks and the door swings open.

"Mrs. Smith, I see you're awake. How are you?" Dr. Lucerto gives Nathan a worried look.

"Can I go home?" I ask.

"Not today," he says. "Mr. Smith, may I see you outside?"

"This involves me, say what you want here." I panic, thinking of my last involuntary stay at the psych ward.

Dr. Lucerto looks at Nathan, who nods his head.

"Very well. We will need to increase the dosage of her medication. They seem to be wearing off quicker. Has anything changed in her life recently?" He talks directly to Nathan as if I'm not there.

"We just got married. The stress of the wedding may have caused this," says Nathan as he texts someone. "Sorry, that was my mother. She's very worried."

Betsy didn't give a shit about me. She is worried about Nathan's campaign. If it were up to her, she'd lock me up and throw away the key.

"Shall we increase the dosage?" asks Dr. Lucerto.

"No," I scream.

"Please calm down," says Dr. Lucerto.

"I'll be better," I say. I'm not sure why I say anything. My pleading doesn't move Nathan.

"Let's give it a day or two," says Dr. Lucerto. Nathan nods

his head and tells me he has to talk to his campaign staff.

"I'm sorry," I say.

Nathan doesn't turn to acknowledge me. "It's okay."

"I'm sorry," I repeat as he leaves.

BETSY VISITS ME the next day. She orders the staff to leave us alone. She hands me an envelope and a pen.

"What's this for?" I ask.

"Annulment papers," she says.

"Did Nathan see this?" I try to get up, but days of confinement have weakened my muscles.

"He doesn't want to leave you with nothing, even though you don't deserve any kindness. He wants to offer you a parting gift." Betsy opens the document to Exhibit A.

"Parting gift?" I ask.

"He asked his grandfather to break his trust." She tightens her lips.

"I don't want it," I tell her.

"This was to go towards Nathan's presidential campaign when the time came, but he wants you to be taken care of. He doesn't think you'll recover. He told me about your other episodes." She flips to the last page.

"I don't want it." I grab the document and throw it across the room.

"Don't make me get the doctor." She smirks and walks to the door.

"Stop." I ease myself up.

"If you love Nathan, you'll take this money. He won't be able to leave you, otherwise." She hands the documents to me again.

"Exorcism by blood," whispers my mother's voice in my ear.

"No, Mother," I whisper back.

"Don't call me Mother," says Betsy.

"Do it," orders my mother.

At first a flutter, anger rises from my bowels and slowly creeps into my mouth. The unwanted invader weighs down my tongue, refusing to leave. Not until I let out a cry, does it fall out into the universe, evaporating into the cold, dry air. Rancid steam heats my throat as if anger was not finished with me, and I clamp my teeth to hold it down.

My arms hurl uncontrollably, and I accidentally punch Betsy in the face. She shrieks. I realize she'll call the nurses on me, and I put the pillow over her head to shut her up. When she stops struggling, I change clothes with her and take her car keys.

Escaping won't be hard. Betsy asked the staff to leave the floor so we wouldn't be interrupted. Her father built this hospital so he could hide his first wife away and marry his mistress. Family money has kept this place open for years. Whatever Betsy said was law.

I run down the stairs. Every floor is locked except the fourth. I walk quickly but cautiously down the corridors. I pass the neonatal unit. The babies seem to be watching me.

I have to stop Kathy from ruining Nathan. Whatever political differences we have, he has always tried to look past my faults, just like Tommy did. As I reach the exit door, I see a boy. I pause as I study his Agnes Scott sweatshirt. He places something cold in my hand.

"What's this?" I ask.

The boy walks away. I look down and it's a knife. I run with it to the parking garage. As usual, Kathy has parked in the handicap spot.

"I can afford the ticket," she always bragged.

I pull out of the garage as the police arrive. I assume they have found her body.

NATHAN IS BACK at Agnes Scott again. He wants to make up for the fiasco that happened last time. I see him at the podium— confident, handsome, better off without me. He concludes his speech and walks off the stage.

Kathy approaches him and whispers something in his ear. I run to him, wanting to save him. He laughs at whatever she says. I push Kathy away from him.

"I'm here to save you, darling," I scream.

"What are you doing here?" he asks.

"She's trying to destroy you," I yell.

"Who? My mother?" He looks at Kathy.

"No, her!" I grab Kathy. "She wants me to suffer. She wants to destroy your campaign."

"I don't know who you are." She ducks behind Nathan.

"Like hell, you don't. You're Tommy's sister."

"Tommy who?" she asks.

"Shut up, you were my college roommate."

"I'm a volunteer. I've never met you."

"She's lying. She asked me to give her the names of the people who bombed the abortion clinic."

Nathan winces.

"Michelle moved here from Dallas to work on the campaign," he explains.

"I've called the police," says another campaign worker.

"Miss, we need to get you to a hospital," says one of the guards.

"I have to stop this woman," I say.

"From doing what?" asks Nathan.

"She's out to destroy us," I say.

"Michelle, show her your driver's license," says Nathan.

I rip it out of her trembling hands.

"Michelle Dawson," I say aloud.

The clawing begins again.

Impressions

The man is asleep in the chair at the coffee shop again. The stained, beige blanket wrapped around him only exposes the top of his head.

This is the third day I've watched him, hoping to make eye contact. I've asked the regular customers about him, but no one seems to know anything. They act as if they don't notice that he's sleeping in a public place. It's as if this is normal behavior.

He stirs and I slide to the edge of my seat, ready to jump up and speak to him. It's a false alarm. His head tilts to his left and he nestles himself deeper into the seat.

I'm supposed to be finishing a project for work this morning. My job is to transfer the addresses from the company's database into a manageable spreadsheet for our client. My boss is Mandy Dixon, Vice President and the top producer at Creative Futures, Atlanta's largest life insurance company. She only gives me very simple tasks. I try to convince myself it's because she's a bit of a micromanager but it's probably because I only have a GED.

Mandy has an MBA but the others gossip about how she landed the job. Within months of arriving at our office as an executive assistant, she became the CEO's right hand person. A few months after that, she was appointed to Vice President of Corporate Accounts. She's basically hand-fed the CEO's client list. We all wonder if she could make seven figures if she had to dig up her own business.

The other admins say Mandy is the CEO's mistress, though I've never seen one inappropriate look between them. In my opinion, they act more like father and daughter. I'm sucked into the slut-shaming at times, but I keep telling myself I'd rather be hitched to a rising star than be ogled by the other producers at the firm.

I've been told none of the guys wanted to hire me. Everyone was surprised when Mandy said she'd take me. She's always so perfectly dressed in designer suits. I couldn't name one of the brands she wears. Most of my clothes are from Ross or Target, which is a hell of a step up from where my parents got our stuff from when I was a kid. I guess that's why it doesn't really bother me when the girls turn their noses up when I walk into a meeting. And no one ever invites me to lunch or drinks.

I should be grateful for what I have, but I wonder what I could have been if I had all the advantages Mandy had. We're the same age and I'm sitting in a coffee shop staring at a homeless man while she's selling million-dollar life insurance policies.

Every morning, I tell Mandy I need a solid two hours of quiet, uninterrupted time at the coffee shop to make the project perfect. She rolls her eyes at me but doesn't say I can't go.

An hour and a half into my temporary escape today, I still can't concentrate. Every time the man twitches, I jump. Every toss and turn makes me anxious.

I ask the barista if he knows who the man is. He says it's one of the "local men" who come in here. No one knows his name. He adds that the manager lets him sleep there in the mornings and I shouldn't worry about it.

My two-hour outing is nearing an end. I text Mandy and say I need more time and I'll be back after lunch. My phone beeps several times, but I don't have the nerve to read her replies.

The man moves again. This time, he takes a sip of his coffee and a bite of something from a crinkled paper bag. Did he get it from a shelter? It looks like one of the lunch bags they hand out at some soup kitchens. I wasn't aware of any around here.

I watch his head as he chews. I know what he's feeling. Should I buy him something to eat? What if he's allergic to what I give him?

I remember taking a bite out of that awful block of government cheese my parents brought back from the food bank. It didn't matter that I'm lactose intolerant. I was hungry. I didn't care about the consequences. The next several hours were spent in the bathroom, where I hoped I could shit away my awful life instead of emptying my insides.

The man takes another sip of coffee and stands up. He folds up his blanket into a tiny square and crams it into a backpack. He throws the backpack over his shoulder and heads to the door. He tries to leave but I'm blocking his path.

"Oh, excuse me ma'am. I'm late for work." He smiles at me.

I stare at his navy outfit. It's crinkled. I can't quite figure out what it is.

He waits for me to move.

I try to make sense of what's he's wearing.

"Have a blessed day," he says. He nods his head and steps around me.

I watch him walk across the parking lot and down the sidewalk.

A woman approaches me and whispers, "I know, he's cute. He's a doctor at Kennestone Hospital. We all come here to watch him, too."

My face reddens.

"A doctor?" I ask.

"Didn't you notice he was wearing scrubs? He volunteers at the homeless shelter on Cherokee Street every morning. Actually, he funds it. He comes here to take a nap before he heads to work."

"A doctor." My stomach rumbles.

"Oh dear, can I buy you a sandwich?" asks the woman. "I don't want to pry, but it looks like you need some help."

You Are Needed Everywhere

Mother named my sister Taiyo. In Japanese, it means "sun." She was born during a happy time in my mother's life. She named me Kaze, which means "wind." I suppose I was a representation of the things she wanted to somehow float away. By the time I was born, my American father had already shipped back home. He told her he would keep in touch. She knew it was a promise most GIs broke, returning home to their blonde, blue-eyed brides.

My maternal grandparents never accepted my mother's half-breeds. Our light hair and frog-like eyes frightened them. They said the good energy was stripped from our heads, and our eyes pulsated as if they were constantly searching for something.

"Lost spirits without a home always try to steal the souls from good people," my grandmother would tell my mother. "You must take them far from here."

No one talks about how we ended up in Hapeville, Georgia. Mother said she didn't know anyone here, though I assume my father had mentioned his hometown during their five years together. Sometimes, I think she wanted to return me to him, the one thing he left behind that she didn't want.

My sister embraced our new homeland, throwing away all traces of our secret shame. She returned home from her first day of school and announced her name was now "Tanya." We were to address her as such, and she would not answer to Taiyo anymore. Although she was no longer called the sun, she remained the center of Mother's universe.

As soon as we could afford the tuition, she sent Tanya to a private school. Unlike me, she was a model student. She was the valedictorian and class president. Confident, she was our mother's daughter.

Mother spoke only broken English when we landed in the Deep South. She, like Tanya, hoped to attain the American dream. She signed up for a conversational English class. There, she met Lisa Liu. Lisa owned a Chinese-style, chicken wing shack near some rundown factories in East Pointe. When the plants shut down, she moved her operation to Buford Highway, the Asian mecca of Atlanta.

Lisa told Mother to do what other Asians with a limited vocabulary did to survive—open a Chinese restaurant. She brought Mother into her circle of entrepreneurs and, more importantly, let her join the Lottery Club. Every month, ten women deposited five thousand dollars with Lisa. Each member took a turn receiving fifty thousand dollars to improve their business. The first deposit was hard to scrape together but she did it. And with Lisa's blessing, Mother became an important member of the business community.

At first, customers chuckled when Mother said "flied lice" instead of fried rice, and "bejeteble" soup instead of vegetable. But over time, people grew to love her and helped her learn the language. Her hole-in-the wall restaurant next to a gas station moved to a shopping center anchored by a Winn-Dixie supermarket. Then, with the help of the Lottery Club money, she moved to her own free-standing building on the main road a few years later.

I've worked at Chinese Delight ever since I was a child. No one seemed to glance twice at a child running through the restaurant. Some found it adorable when I brought out the pu pu platter that was almost as big as I was. Washing dishes started at age ten, prep work began at fourteen, and finally, I started cooking when I turned sixteen.

Tanya left Hapeville soon after graduation and moved into student housing at Emory University in Atlanta. She's an insurance defense attorney now. She married a Korean plastic surgeon six years ago. Their grand wedding took place at the

Atlanta Botanical Gardens. Of their three hundred guests, only Mother was from our side of the family. Everyone else was from Dr. Kim's side, or one of their many lawyer or doctor friends. I couldn't go because I had to run the restaurant.

Three months ago, Tanya had her second child. She's been hinting that she wants Mother to move in with them. Someone has to watch the children while Tanya defends insurance companies against the little people and her husband gives Americanized eyelids to Asian women.

Tanya's older child attends the prestigious Woodward Academy. Even though the attorney and doctor can afford the annual twenty-thousand-dollar tuition, Mother promises to provide the money every fall. "Children should be nurtured," she tells me as she writes the check.

Mother is in Atlanta visiting her golden child and heavenly grandchildren now. She calls me from Tanya's Tudor-style house in Buckhead, which is a stone's throw away from the Governor's mansion. Each morning before the prep, she reminds me of what needs to be done. Given that she hasn't cooked in the last ten years, I roll my eyes.

My silence disturbs her. "Are you mocking me?" she asks.

"Okay, okay," I say. "I won't forget to wash the cabbage before I cook it."

"No respect," she says.

"Sorry, Mother." I know I will pay for this when she returns.

"Do you think you can handle the restaurant for a few days?" Mother asks me on the phone.

I talk in circles, not saying whether she should stay there or come back. Whatever I say will be wrong in the end. "You are needed everywhere," I tell her.

"I'll be home Sunday," she says before she hangs up. She acts as though we are hundreds of miles apart. Buckhead is only a thirty-minute drive from Hapeville. In Mother's mind, the two worlds can't touch.

"Is Mrs. Tanaka here?" asks an unfamiliar voice.

Startled by the strange smell of cedar and cigarettes, I whirl around armed with my cleaver. Mother warned me about leaving the back door unlocked. There have been robberies around the neighborhood lately, and she says it's only a matter of time until we are hit. Perhaps she is right not to trust me to run things, after all.

The man throws up his arms. "Whoa. Whoa. I'm just here to drop off the extra chicken wings Mrs. Tanaka ordered."

"Sorry, she's not here." Mother deals with the ordering, so I wasn't expecting a delivery. She doesn't trust me with "brainy" things.

"Can you sign for it? I'm running late." He is thin, his dragon tattoo peeking out of his tight, black shirt. I stare at it, wondering if he has a fascination with Asian culture.

"Sure." I notice five boxes stacked near the back counter. I look down to see if the delivery man scuffed up Mother's pristine floors. "She ordered all these wings?"

"Super Bowl weekend," he says.

"Right. I forgot all about it." Now I know I shouldn't be running things.

"I'll be here on Wednesday with the regular order. Will she be back?" He shuffles his feet, then lifts up each foot to inspect the floor. I assume Mother has scolded him for tracking dirt into her kitchen before.

"She'll be back," I say. I study his high-top Converse sneakers. I haven't seen anyone wear those since I was in high school. I wonder if he is younger than I am but then I see some creases around his eyes. Mother says lines around the face aren't always a true indicator of age, especially in full-blooded Caucasians.

"Cool. I'm Josh." He extends his hand.

"I'm Kari." I haven't said that name since high school. Mother still calls me Kaze, and the staff calls me Ms. T.

His hand is rough but warm. "I'll see you next week."

"Okay." I follow to lock the door behind him. He turns and

crashes into me.

"Do you want to get a drink with me later?" He doesn't move from the spot where we smacked into each other.

I look up at him, stepping back. "We close pretty late."

"Eleven, right?" he asks.

"Yes, then clean-up afterwards. We don't leave until midnight." I exhale quickly when he looks away.

"No worries. The bars close at three." Even with a step between us, I can feel his breath on my face.

"I shouldn't. I have to open up the restaurant early." I look at the floor. I am twenty-six years old and never been asked out on a date. It is beyond embarrassing. How would I act with a man? What would we talk about?

"Just one drink. I promise." He grins.

"I guess it couldn't hurt." Mother will be back in a few days. I won't be able to go out again after her return.

"I'll be back at midnight," he says.

"Make it twelve-thirty. I don't want the employees to talk." I blush, thinking how stupid I sound.

"Cool." He pushes the dolly out the door.

I lock the door behind him. I trudge through the rest of the day, glancing at the clock above the walk-in cooler. The other cook has to bang his spatula on the side of his wok a few times to get my attention. I nod a silent apology but then remember Mother telling me to let the staff know who is in charge. "Never admit you're wrong," she always says.

Mateo, the bus boy, won't leave at night until I'm safely in my car. Mother is always afraid things will be taken from her, and she is overly cautious as a result. But in this case, she is right.

"Señorita, I mean, Miss." Mother has lectured the staff about speaking Spanish, and Mateo knows she will go crazy if she hears he has disobeyed her. Even we stopped speaking Japanese the moment our feet touched Georgia soil. "We're in America, and we must adapt," was drilled into our heads.

What the employees don't know is that Mother has an underground safe. The fireproof six by six space holds her money—all of it. She's been stashing it for years. The IRS and the bank only know about half of what the restaurant takes in.

"When I die, the grandchildren inherit it," she tells me.

"That's fine, Mother. They can have it all," I reassure her. I will be relieved to hand it all over. It is and always has been beneath Tanya to be in the food service industry. She will sell the building and stash the money away in her precious children's trust funds. Then I will be free.

I finger the small bit of cash I have left over from my last paycheck. I wouldn't dare take money without Mother's permission. She only started paying me a few years ago, when the accountant told her it was tax deductible. And since she was paying some of the illegal workers under the table, she had to show a believable number of salaried employees.

Josh's delivery truck pulls up next to my car. He jumps out and tries to open my car door. It's locked, so he taps on the window.

"I'm trying to be a gentleman," he says.

I push the door open. "Sorry."

"Would you rather follow me?" he asks.

"Yes, if that's okay." Reflux gurgles up my throat.

"Cool. It's only twenty minutes from here." He closes my door.

His truck crawls down the highway then exits into the trendy part of Atlanta. He stops in front of an old Wal-Mart, which has been renovated into a local gathering place. I pull up next to him. Still deciding if he is a serial killer or not, I sit in my locked car.

Again, he tries to open my door. "Coming in?" he asks.

I open the door. "Just one drink."

"Just one drink," he says. He grabs my hand and smiles.

I pull back, my face flushed. I don't want him to know I've never been out on a date before.

"Come on, the bar closes soon." He doesn't seem to notice my awkwardness—or he has chosen not to acknowledge it.

Josh pushes me inside. "It's a bookstore, coffee shop, and bar. Isn't it cool?"

"How long has this been here?" I ask.

"A while." He sits down at the bar and hands me a drink menu.

My heart is beating out of my chest. I have to leave before I embarrass myself any further.

"What do you want to drink?" he asks.

I shrug my shoulders. I can't tell him I've never had a drink, other than the plum wine Mother let me taste at Tanya's high school graduation party. I don't think that's on the menu here.

"There are five beers on tap, beer in bottles, wine, and liquor. There are a few fruity drinks too, but the bartenders don't like to make them." He points to the choices on the daily drink menu.

"Wine," I say. I assume wine is the same everywhere.

"Josh, I see you brought a new friend." The waitress taps her order pad. "What would you like?"

"Wine," I say.

"Which one?" she asks.

I flip the cardboard stock over and over again.

"Give her a Merlot. I'll have whatever's on draft."

The waitress nods her head and walks away.

I look down at my lap and try to slow my breath.

"So, what do you do for fun?"

"I'm always at the restaurant," I say. I wonder how long this conversation will go on before Josh wants to leave. The only conversations I have are about late bus boys, cranky wait staff, and why customers order a dish then substitute all the ingredients out of it.

"Do you like movies? Do you read?" He points at the bookshelves.

"I watch whatever show is on from midnight to two." I still

haven't looked at him.

"The new Daniel Craig movie is out. Do you want to go see it tomorrow?" He leans over and tilts his head down to meet mine.

"Tomorrow?" I was surprised he wanted to see me again.

"You can give me your answer at the end of the night," he says.

The drinks arrive. I swish the wine around in my mouth like I've seen people do in movies, then swallow. It burns my throat. I almost cough but I don't want to embarrass myself, so I try hard to suppress it. I finish it, and Josh orders me another one. The second glass goes down smoother, and faster. My head starts to spin.

"I should go," I say.

"You sure you can drive?"

"I'm okay," I say.

He walks me to my car and presses against me. I try to step back but I'm already backed up against the car handle.

"Are we going to the movie?" He strokes my cheek.

I nod. He leans in further and places a warm kiss on my lips. I close my eyes, letting the moment wash over me. It's more enjoyable than the time Lisa's son, Andy, crammed his tongue into my mouth when our mothers left us alone to go on their monthly gambling trip to Tunica, Mississippi.

"I'll see you tomorrow," he says.

I sit in the car for a while and notice Mother has called me three times. I shudder, knowing I'll need to lie to her in the morning.

Mother calls the restaurant at ten, sharp. She demands to know where I was last night. I tell her I was tired, exhausted from being here without her guidance. She accepts my explanation and goes down her checklist.

"Did they make the wing delivery yesterday?" she asks.

"Yes, yes." I keep my voice steady so she doesn't detect nervousness.

"Don't let that man cheat you," she says.

"The produce delivery is here; I have to go," I say. "You have nothing to worry about."

"I'll call back later." She hangs up.

I put my phone in my apron. I pull it back out to make sure she hung up, and that she can't hear my uneven breathing.

After closing, Mateo wants to see me exit the parking lot before he goes. "Mrs. Tanaka will kill me if something went wrong."

"Don't worry. I'll take the blame." I pat him on the shoulder and get into my car. I lock the door. "See, you have nothing to worry about," I say through the closed window.

Mateo looks back several times before he is out of sight. Josh arrives as soon as Mateo disappears.

"There's a new drive-in. The movie already started but we can still get in. Do you want to ride with me?" He adjusts his hat and smiles.

"Sure," I say. I climb into his truck, wiping the sweat from my upper lip. The front of the cab has one long, leather seat and if I wasn't wearing my seatbelt, I would slide into Josh when he turned left.

He pulls into a space and adjusts the radio to the right frequency. I don't recognize any of the actors in the movie. Since it's halfway over, I can't get into the story.

"Do you want some popcorn?" he asks.

I shake my head. My hands are frozen even though it's unseasonably warm this January. I place them under my legs for warmth.

"Do you want a blanket? I've got one in the back." Josh pats my knee.

I pull my coat tightly around me. "I'm okay."

"Don't worry, it's clean," he says before he jumps in the back. He pulls the blanket off of a thin mattress. My heart thunders under my coat. All of the crime shows I've been watching flood into my head. I wonder if he's going to keep me hostage back there.

"Really, it's okay," I squeak.

"Here," he says as he wraps me up.

I grab my purse strap, ready to run. "Thanks."

He turns forward and watches the movie. My eyes bounce back and forth from his slight movements to the screen. He laughs. I twitch.

"You okay? Do you want to leave?" His eyes twinkle.

"I should get home. Two late nights in a row isn't good. I'm going to be really tired tomorrow." I clench my fists, ready to hit him if he attacks me.

"I get it. I have deliveries out of state tomorrow. How about we get together Sunday night?" He slides closer to me.

"No, my mother will be back, and I won't be able to . . ." I stop, hearing how childish I sound. He may not know exactly how old I am, but he knows I'm well over eighteen.

He touches my face with the side of his hand. "Don't you get any days off?"

I shake my head.

"So, is this the last time I'll see you?" he asks.

"Yes," I say. I want to explain why I can't see him anymore, but since he's interacted with Mother several times, I'm sure he already knows the reason. "I'm sorry. I can't go out with you again."

He holds the sides of my face and leans in to kiss me. My hands fall and I push them into the leather seat, bracing myself. I know I should tell him to stop but I don't. I can't.

His hands slide down my breasts and he fingers my nipples. I lean into him and the blanket falls from my shoulder. His lips caress the back of my ears and his hands are now between my legs. I moan.

"Do you want to go in the back?" he asks.

I am out of breath. I wonder if this is how Mother felt when my father seduced her. I can't help to think about him. Mother says she hasn't seen him since he left Japan. I wonder if Josh will leave me like that.

His warm fingers graze my skin as he unbuttons my blouse. Embarrassed, I sit up.

"Do you want me to stop?" he asks.

"I don't know," I say.

"It's cool," he says. He looks deep into my eyes. "The movie will be over soon."

"Uh-huh," I say.

He takes my hand and leads me to the back of the truck. I lie back and he undresses me. I don't tell him I've never had sex before. I close my eyes until it's over. I tell him we can't do this again. Mother would not approve. He doesn't argue.

After he drops me off at the restaurant, I sit in my car for over an hour, kicking myself for not saying no. I go home and take a long, hot bath. Mother has called several times and I know I will pay the price when she returns.

Mother arrives Sunday before the dinner rush. She is happy, ripe from visiting her good daughter. She lets the night go by without confrontation.

"We will talk tomorrow," she says. "I don't want you to spoil my mood. You know I like a whole day of uninterrupted happiness. Unpleasantness can always start tomorrow."

I nod.

The next morning, she questions Mateo several times in her office. He doesn't look at me as he walks by. "Sorry, amiga," he mumbles, as he flies by my work station.

And yet, she says nothing.

Josh brings the regular delivery on Wednesday morning. As Mother signs the order, she studies him. He squirms, his hand outstretched for the clipboard. Mother holds it close to her chest and smirks.

"Everything okay while I'm gone?" she asks.

"Yes, ma'am." Josh rocks back and forth on his heels.

She lets the silence engulf both of us. "See you next week."

"The clipboard?" he asks.

"Oh, yes. I mustn't take what isn't mine." It may be my guilty conscience, but I think she's looking at me.

Josh darts out the back door. "Thanks!"

"He's married," she says.

"Who?" I ask innocently.

"The American," she says.

"How do you know?" I ask.

"I know what a married man looks like," she says.

I escape to the cooler, pretending to look for the marinated chicken. The following Wednesday, another delivery man brings our meat. I suppose Mother has complained about Josh. She has made sure she won't have to see him again.

IT'S SPRING AND Mother wants to discuss the seasonal menu. She talks about green beans for a minute, then launches into talk of Tanya. Mother has decided to move in with her and the doctor.

I've had my own visit with a doctor. After weeks of nausea, he confirmed that I'm pregnant. I cried so much he wanted to hospitalize me. I refused to go. His nurse went through the options with me. I told her I'd think about it. I've been in a daze since then. Mother hasn't noticed. She's been busy, getting ready for her big move.

"I'm ready to raise a second generation of happy, ambitious children," she says.

She informs me that I will run the restaurant and help run Lisa's restaurant as well. Lisa's husband stole the Lottery Club money and lost it in a poker game. Mother offered to cover the missing funds in exchange for Lisa's restaurant on Buford Highway.

"Lisa went back to Hong Kong, but she asked me to keep Andy," she says. Not having children to tie me down, she says I can divide my time between here and overseeing Andy at his location.

"You have to keep the restaurant going for all the loyal

customers," she says.

I try to hide my shaking hands behind my back.

"I will be back once a week to check the receipts." She looks up from the computer screen. "You sick again?"

I slide down the wall and put my head between my knees. I try to hold in what little I had for lunch.

"Go to the emergency clinic and see the nurse there. Hurry back before the dinner rush." She motions me to leave her office.

My knees freeze, but I'm drenched in sweat from the waist up. I try to stand but my legs are gelatin.

"I already went to the doctor. I'm pregnant, Mother," I say.

Her face puckers. "Who is the father?"

I shake my head.

"You can't keep it," she barks.

"I want the baby," I say.

"You always said you didn't want a family." She keeps checking the menu.

"Two generations of unwanted children under your roof would have been unbearable." I stare at my feet, which are growing out of my loafers.

"Kaze, no one said you couldn't be happy," she says.

"Nothing happens without your permission, Mother," I say.

She drops her pencil and her disappointment pours over me. "Obviously, that's not true."

"I have decided to name the baby Amora," I say.

"Amora?" she asks. "Is that Spanish?"

"Yes, it means 'love.'" My lip trembles, and I look up from her immaculately mopped floor.

"Will you tell the father?" she asks.

"Yes, he deserves to know," I say.

"What if he doesn't want you or the baby?" she asks.

"He will have to tell me to my face," I say. "I won't let him run away and abandon his responsibility."

"And if he's married?" she asks.

"That's another thing he will have to say in person," I say.

For the first time in my life, Mother looks away first. She closes her eyes. "So, you won't be running the restaurants after the baby comes?" she asks.

I shake my head.

"Amora," she says.

"Amora," I say back. A love I can hold, not one that floats away in the wind.

The Winner

The woman pushes the baby stroller into the casino again.
Keith, the floor boss, yells, "Twenty-one and over!"

She may have heard it one too many times because it doesn't faze her.

"Get her out of here, Sally," Keith says to me.

"Why me?" I ask. "I'm out of the counseling business."

"I can't throw a woman out of here. I'd look like an ass." He sticks out his lower lip like a little boy. I suppose he's younger than my son, but he's still well into his thirties.

"Grow a pair, Keith," I say as I walk over to her. The woman's husband/boyfriend/baby-daddy isn't around this time. The homely man usually watches the baby while the woman plays her quarter slots. The clink of each coin made them both wince. Periodically, he'd try to coax her to leave, but he couldn't pry her away until she'd lost all their money.

Lucky Lou's is probably the only place that would allow someone to bring a baby into a casino. It is a relic of the 1950's, decaying far from the Las Vegas strip. The stench of every cigarette smoked in here is trapped in the faded carpet and droopy ceiling tiles.

The slot machines are as outdated as the décor. They don't take players' cards like the ones at the newer casinos. Our older clientele drop their dirty quarters in before pulling the lever, which often sticks halfway down. They complain about it, but they keep coming back.

The woman sees me approach and throws me a fake smile. "Hi, I'm Abby." She pushes the stroller into a space between the wall and the slot machine.

"Do you know that you can't bring a baby in here? It's the law." I wait to see if she's going to give me a rational response.

"Can you keep an eye on him for a few minutes then?" She exaggerates a smile when I fold my arms.

"Young lady, I have to serve drinks."

"Oh, please. I don't have anyone to watch him. My husband left after our last visit here. I don't know any of our neighbors at Desert Arms." Abby slumps forward and she grasps the handle of the stroller. "Sorry, I haven't eaten today."

I look at my watch. It's two in the afternoon and I wonder if she's fed the baby. "Maybe we can watch him for a little while," I say as I pull the stroller out of its cramped quarters.

Abby smiles and turns her attention to her machine.

I've seen this many times in my thirty-plus years serving drinks in Sin City. Nothing I say is going to stop this girl from gambling. It's a sickness that's hard to shake. Someone has to hit rock bottom to stop. And sometimes even then, people try to dig a little deeper.

"I think he's hungry," I say to the other waitresses. They take turns pinching his cheeks and rubbing his belly.

"I'll get some mashed potatoes and peas off the buffet." I ask one of the waitresses to keep an eye on him. I can't help but smile. It's been a long time since I smelled the innocence of a baby. Once a mother, always a mother.

Keith grabs my arm. "I told you to throw her out of here."

"Keith, you know I don't let a man put his hands on me anymore." I push him and he slinks back to the gaming tables.

Around half past four, Mike and Nina show up. Nina squeezes the baby's cheeks. "Boy or girl?" she asks.

"Boy." My stomach churns. Children are so unsafe in this world.

"Whose baby is it?" asks Nina.

"That lady back there," I say.

"Kids are bad luck," says Mike, smoothing out his beard.

"Mike's superstitious. Same flannel shirt, jeans, shoes for every game. He wore the same pair of underwear the entire week of last year's Texas Hold 'Em Tournament at The

Mirage." She laughs. "Gamblers are all the same."

"Yeah," I say. No matter how long I'm here, I'll always be amazed some people's lack of self-awareness. Nina is a gambler herself—not a very good one, but a gambler nonetheless. These days, she's more of a hanger-on.

Mike is her first, third, and current husband. No matter what shit goes sideways between them, it dies down, and they get back together again.

"Do you have kids?" she asks.

I hesitate. No one here knows anything about me. I've made sure of that.

"My daughter's twenty-five now," she announces as if we don't know the story.

"No kids?" she asks again.

"A son," I say. The words seem false. I haven't acknowledged him in three decades.

"Do you see him often?" she asks.

"No, I don't." Thankfully, the baby fusses.

"Bring us some Cokes when you get a chance," says Mike.

"Sure, sweetie." My eyes well up thinking of Sammy. My dear little boy. When the judge, who attended our church, awarded custody to the great Pastor Leach, Sammy stood silently at his father's side. His small hands twitched, as if he wanted to reach out to me, but his father gripped his shoulder. Sammy winced and held his breath. The guards dragged me out of the courthouse and I never saw Sammy again. I told myself that Pastor wouldn't hurt him, and that Sammy wouldn't turn into a monster.

Abby stumbles over to me, breaking me out of my memories. She grabs the stroller and pushes it into the brightly lit Vegas night.

"She didn't even say thank you," says Nina.

"She's too far gone. We'll see her again, though." I watch Abby's silhouette disappear down the cracked sidewalk.

MIKE IS STILL at the poker table when I arrive for my morning shift. He sucks down the last of his cigarette and gulps the remains of his soda. Mike doesn't drink liquor anymore—not since his last breakup from Nina.

A few years ago, Nina showed up here and they had a crazy fight in the men's room. Keith had to call the police. As the officer tried to break them apart, Nina knocked out Mike's front teeth with one of her stilettos.

"You slept with my daughter!" she shrieked.

"Ma'am, how old is your daughter?" asked the officer.

"Twenty-one," she wailed.

"Oh." The officer stood down after finding out it wasn't a child molestation case. "Ma'am I'm going to have to arrest you."

"Take me in before I kill this bastard," she said. Mike didn't press charges, so she walked the next day.

As Mike tells it, the daughter still comes around for the holidays and everything is normal between them. Nina's only worries these days are the ups and downs of gambling life.

Nina arrives an hour into my shift. "Hey, ladies. He still at it?"

"It's heads up with Dr. Ken," I say. Dr. Ken Lee was a dentist from Biloxi. He used to gamble Friday through Sunday nights, then return to his practice early Monday morning. Sunday then became Monday, then Tuesday. He started losing patients. I heard there was a malpractice suit. I'd learned all about Ken Lee when his wife, Kim, blurted everything out during a drunken rage.

"Shit. I'll just sit over here. I don't want to rattle him. Rum and Coke." Nina takes a slow sip. The only way she can drink is behind Mike's back.

Kim's shouting interrupts my conversation with Nina. She's at the blackjack table again. She keeps looking at Dr. Ken's table, itching to go over there. Kim tries now and again to play cards with the big boys. I usually scoot away before she has to fold her hand. When she receives a bad deal, she crumples or tears up the cards. She once ruined seven decks of cards in one game before she was escorted out.

The tiny Korean has been kicked out of here more than anyone else since the casino opened, or at least while I've been working here. She can whoop any bouncer's ass. The other waitresses and I laughed when the police had to remove her because three casino guards couldn't control her.

"My people have been invaded by the Chinese and Japanese, and they couldn't defeat us. You can't keep us down." It's her fighting chant. Every time she says it, we all roll our eyes.

"*Micheossuh,*" some of the other Koreans call her. It means "crazy" in Korean and it fits her.

Gamblers never learn—win at poker, lose it at the house games. Always hopeful, they return to accomplish what no one has ever done and beat the house.

Abby appears from nowhere and strolls right up to Nina and me. "Can you watch him again?"

"No, you know you can't keep doing this," I warn her. Abby scans the room for her lucky machine.

"It's alright, I'll watch him," says Nina.

"It's not healthy for the baby with all this smoke. Go home." I look away.

"Please. I don't have anyone to watch him. I need to make rent money. I pawned my wedding ring already. I know the machine's going to hit soon. I can feel it." She shakes in her oversized clothes.

"Girl, no one gets rich on the slots. I'll teach you how to play poker." Nina smiles at Abby.

"Really?" Abby and I both blurt out the question.

"After Mike gets through this game. Go ahead and play your slots until then." Nina downs her drink.

Abby lets go of the stroller.

"What's his name?" asks Nina.

"Billy," says Abby. She gives the stroller a slight push

towards us and leaves.

"Do you know her story?" asks Nina.

"Just that she used to show up with the husband but now he's gone. I've seen it a thousand times before."

Nina's top lip quivers. "We've all fucked up once."

"Yes, we have," I say.

"Tell me about your kid, Sally."

"He's not a kid anymore. Probably has kids of his own." I sit on the stool next to Nina, catching my breath.

"When's the last time you saw him?" She rattles her glass to the bartender.

"Over thirty years," I say.

"What happened?" She slams her third drink and moans.

I shake my head.

"It's alright. We all have a story. Wouldn't it be good to finally let it out?" She points to her glass. "Another one."

I shrug and the bartender hands her another one.

"Do you think she brought any food for Billy?" asks Nina.

I shake my head. "I'll get something off the buffet."

"He sure is quiet."

"I guess he's used to entertaining himself. You sure you can watch him?"

"I'll keep this little guy company until you get back," she says with her back to Billy.

Is Billy better off with Nina or with Abby? Scurvy, second-hand smoke, or addiction—this kid doesn't have a chance.

I think about Nina's question. Would I feel unburdened if I talked about Sammy? I've pushed it down so deep inside my heart for so long, I don't think I could dig it back out. I'm afraid if I let it go, it will get ugly.

"I'm only a man," he'd say before he hit me. "I'm only a man."

When I filed a police report, the Sheriff showed up at church with his wife. While he went and consoled Pastor, the wife lectured me about ruining a community.

"Do you know how many people he's helped? Do you think this town is going to let you ruin him? He'll mellow out. Just bide your time." That was the end of the investigation.

She was right. Every important citizen attended our church. No one was going to let me get away with such a betrayal. And when they took my son away from me, I left Atlanta to start over.

WHEN I ARRIVE at the buffet, the penny-slot grannies are holding up the line. The five dollar all-you-can-eat buffet draws in all walks of life, from cabbies to young couples to the elderly. The grannies normally come in around eleven in the morning, remark on every item on the buffet, gossip for hours while eating, and settle in at their favorite machines for the rest of the afternoon. And they never tip.

"Fixed income," they say.

I cut in front of them and scoop up some soft foods for Billy.

"Who does she think she is?" one of them asks.

"It's for a baby, you old bird," I throw back at her. I take the plate back to the bar. Nina has placed her glass on Billy's tray and is having an intense conversation with him.

"I'll feed him." She wobbles as she reaches up for the plate.

I put her glass back on the bar. Feeding Billy, Nina looks almost normal.

Keith stops on his way to the pit. "You, too?" he asks Nina.

"Isn't he a doll?" she asks.

"They'll shut us down," he mumbles. He gives me a death stare and huffs off.

"They're so innocent, then they turn into little shits." Nina sings this to Billy as if it's a lullaby. I'm sure he's heard worse.

I walk around the poker tables with watered-down drinks. As the senior waitress, my primary station is the higher rollers area. This term is relative. Lucky Lou's is where whales from the newer casinos come to die. A whale is an extremely high roller who drops hundreds of thousands of dollars, or even millions, at a casino. They are comped suites, given access to limousines, plied with tickets to sold-out shows, and filled with meals by celebrity chefs. They are given anything to keep them from leaving the casino and going to trendier places.

When fortunes are lost for one reason or another, whales drift to older, lesser known establishments. Lucky Lou's is usually the end of the line. We don't have a hotel, but we give discount coupons to a motel down the street. It's close enough for an old whale to stumble to after losing what little he has left.

Dr. Ken and Mike are still at it. Dr. Ken turns the corners of his cards slightly and snaps them back on the table. Mike sits back and looks for a read on the doc's face, but Dr. Ken's dark glasses hide his emotions.

"Check," says Mike.

"Check," echoes Dr. Ken.

Both men flip over their cards. Dr. Ken slams the table. His uncharacteristic blow-up startles the dealer.

"Sorry, can we take a break?" asks Dr. Ken.

The dealer looks at Mike.

"I could use lunch," says Mike.

"Let's come back in an hour," says the dealer. Keith goes over and takes their chips to the safe.

After cursing out the baccarat dealer, Kim sprints to Dr. Ken's side. "You up or down?" she asks.

"Let's eat," he says.

"Just beat the asshole, then we can go to the Commerce Casino. I love how they bring the food to the tables. You never have to leave." She tries to keep up with Dr. Ken as she balances on her six-inch heels.

Dr. Ken nods. He strokes his lucky jade dragon and puts it back in his pocket.

I'll be glad when Kim leaves. She sucks the life out of the room. I've heard some call her an emotional vampire. With half of our clientele near death, it's not good having her around. She seems entitled, always barking orders at me in that cutting tone. She reminds me of Pastor. Maybe that's why I hate her so much.

Nina finishes feeding Billy. Mike is leaning on the bar, holding a pack of cigarettes.

"You have to eat something. You've been at the table for two days."

"A smoke first." He points to the door. "I'll be outside."

"I guess Abby isn't coming back anytime soon," says Nina.

"You go spend time with Mike. I'll take care of him." Billy has fallen asleep. It's a wonder what kids can get used to. All the noises from the machines, yelling, crying, smoke—he's just grown to ignore it all.

"When Mike goes back to the table, let's get a bite to eat." Nina winks and teeters away.

I take Billy outside for some fresh air. He grimaces in the sunlight. But he adapts and begins to smile.

"I'm sorry you have to go through this. But you're better off with us than some nut your mother would have found on the street." He cackles as if he agrees with me.

I have been curious about Sammy. One of the librarians at East Desert Library showed me how to look up information on the Internet. It took me a week to gain the courage to look up the church's website.

Sammy took over his father's church. I see a wife in the photo. Natasha has the same blank stare I used to have. I look closely for bruises, but I assume Sammy would have figured out by now not to hit her face.

Her web page says she counsels women at the halfway house in Jonesboro, a small town south of Atlanta. So she's allowed to leave Sammy's sight. Perhaps she's not going through what I went through. Sammy must be a good man. I hope he's a good man.

When Pastor hit me, Sammy threw his small body between

us. Pastor blamed me for Sammy's defiance and threw his small body into the other room. He never hit him though. That was a small consolation.

"Mama," says Billy.

"Is that your first word? It's a shame that your mother missed it. Let's go back and see if she's out of money yet." I try to turn the stroller around but a large man blocks my path.

"Hey, Sally. How you doing, pretty girl?" All I see is teeth.

"Tank!" I hug his neck, the only part of him I can fully wrap my arms around.

"It's been a while," he says.

"Where have you been hiding?" I ask.

"Back in Memphis. I missed Mr. Richard's cooking. Needed some good fat and salt to sustain all those endless nights."

"I've heard about those oxtails and collards. Poor souls who lose their shirts at your house games still rave about Mr. Richard's cooking. I think he puts a spell on those folks so you can take their money."

Tank's belly jiggles with laughter. "That's our little secret."

I am thankful he isn't offended by my statement.

"Who's this?" he asks. Tank bends down as far as his body will allow.

"Some poor souls can't stay away from here. She keeps bringing the little guy back."

"It's not healthy. Good Lord, it's bad enough for grown folk." Tank shakes his head. "Maybe we should buy him some baby headphones. He shouldn't be exposed to all this noise."

"We're headed back in to see if his mother is ready to go. Dr. Ken and Mike are head to head again. Most of the regulars have been back there watching all day."

"Why do they even play each other? Money just keeps going back and forth between them."

"Some people are gluttons for punishment," I say.

"I guess I'll take a look. There's a game planned for this weekend at the house. Why don't you come down?"

"Me? I'm not a fan of the South."

"Right. Right. Well, let me look at the newbies."

"Okay, Tank. Take care of yourself." I follow the huge men inside.

"Tank!" yells the bartender.

"A couple of ginger ales," says Tank.

"What? I have a special bottle hidden down here for you." The bartender points underneath the bar.

"Thanks, but I need to keep my head clear. I'm scouting for my game. Need a few dudes who are easily parted with their coins." Tank laughs and slaps the bar. His bear claw shakes the cheap foundation.

"You playing?" asks one of the waitresses.

"Yeah, to feel out the talent. I'm gonna lose a grand. See if the baby sharks are hungry." He fishes a wad of bills from his pocket.

"Oh my God, it's Tank Bryant," squeals one of the players. "Can I have your autograph?"

"I guess he's found his mark," Patty whispers to me.

"Who would turn down a chance to play with an ex-NFL player?" I ask.

"Especially one who flashes a Super Bowl ring on each hand," says Patty.

"True," I say. I used to feel sorry for these poor suckers, until they kept going back. Who leaves Vegas to play cards in Memphis? Dumb shits keep getting led into slaughter.

"Your shift is almost over. What are you going to do with the kid?" asks the bartender. He looks at Billy like he's a sack of potatoes I might stash in the back.

"I guess I'll have to let Keith kick Abby out today. She must be winning, though. She's been here a long time." I scan the room for her frail silhouette. She is hunched over, elbows on the ledge of the machine, head leaning into the glow. I tap her on the shoulder. She jumps, glares at me then swirls back around.

She studies the spinning reels. Her head bops as the jangly

music gets louder. Cherry. Cherry. Lemon. "You made me lose," she says.

"My shift is ending in fifteen minutes. You have to take Billy home. No one else is going to watch him." I tap her again.

"I watch him." Sharp, broken English cuts through the dings. Kim looks at us, drink in hand. "I know how it is. I've been kicked out of lots of places because of my daughter."

"You have a kid?" I ask in amazement.

"Yeah, yeah. My mother has her." She shakes her glass at Abby. "Yes or no?"

"Yes," says Abby, without turning around.

Kim hands her glass to me and takes control of the stroller. "No appreciate," she says to Abby and walks away with Billy.

"You're going to let her watch your child?" I ask.

Abby isn't fazed. "She seems okay. She said she has kids."

"You don't know her. As soon as the new pit boss comes on duty, she'll ditch Billy. The only reason she's watching him is because she was thrown off the floor." I lean in closer to Abby, but she doesn't move.

"This machine's going to hit any minute. Then I can go home." She glances at me. "Are we cool now?"

I throw up my arms. "If you don't care, why should I?"

Kim pushes Billy outside. She squats down with a lit cigarette in her mouth, saying something to the bewildered child.

"I'm going home to soak my feet and fall asleep in front of the TV," I tell the bartender.

"Have a good one," he says.

I grab my tips and walk outside. A toothless man is rolling dice next to Billy, and Kim is nowhere to be seen.

"Where's the lady who was watching this baby?" I ask him.

"She gave me five dollars and said the kid's mother will give me another five when she comes out." His stench burns my eyes.

I dig out ten dollars out of my pocket and hand it to him. "Thanks for watching him. I'll take him."

"You shouldn't bring a kid to a casino. You don't know what kind of weirdos hang out here." He smiles and his tongue peeks out of the hole where teeth once had been.

"Thanks again," I say. I wheel Billy back inside.

"How'd you get the kid back?" asks Nina.

"That idiot, Kim, dumped the baby as soon as she could get back on the floor."

"Shouldn't we call the police? It's not right. Who knows who else the mother is leaving the child with? What if he gets molested or kidnapped?"

"Even though she's a poor excuse for a human being, I don't want her to lose Billy. I know it's the worst thing that can happen to a mother."

"Some people deserve it," she says.

"I can't do it." I look at Billy. I know he needs parents who love him, but I can't bring myself to call. I don't want to be responsible for taking away Abby's child.

"You can't do this every day," says Nina. "Do what's best for the kid."

"Let me tell Abby that we might call the cops. Maybe it will scare her into leaving."

"If that makes you feel better," she says. "Leave Billy here in case she goes crazy."

Keith runs towards the bar, panting. "Where's the woman?"

"What woman?" I ask.

"The baby's mother," he says, wiping his forehead.

"Back there," I say, pointing to the back row of slot machines.

"Social services is here. Go get her before we're shut down." His eyes are wide as plates.

I wobble as fast as my thick thighs will allow. I tug on Abby's sleeve. "Sweetie, you have to go."

"It's going to hit. I can't leave." She puts her hand in my face.

"Social services is going to take Billy," I say.

"They always threaten, but they never do it," she says, flatly. Her eyeballs watch the three reels spin around.

I pull her off the stool. She screams all the way back to the bar. Her eyes try to adjust as they focus on humans rather than a glowing machine.

A woman in a gray suit approaches us. She hands Abby her card. "I'm Rosa McDonald from Child and Family Services. Do you know why I'm here? Do you know what your rights are?"

Abby glances at the back wall and studies the person hovering over her lucky machine. "That's my mach . . ."

"Miss, I need to take your child into our custody now. Here's my card. Call that number in the morning." The social worker takes the stroller and walks out of the casino.

Abby squints as Billy disappears into the setting sun. She holds out her arms trying to reach him, but her legs can't let her leave. Her knees buckle and she falls on the dingy carpet. Just as she puts her hands over her ears to block out the ringing of the slot machines, a piercing siren quiets the crowd. Flashing disco lights rotate around the dank room. Someone yells, "I won!"

Sacred Spaces

Freddie always valued the space between our legs more than the space between our ears. "Smart girls don't make me money, sexy girls do," he told us.

Thankfully, he won't be saying anything ever again. One morning, the beer delivery guy found Freddie filleted in the back office. According to the police report, Freddie was stabbed several times. His pants and boxers were around his ankles, and his shirt was on the floor. There was evidence that he was being pleasured before his death, although the DNA evidence couldn't be narrowed down to a single person. There were hundreds of fingerprints and several other types of human samples splattered around the strip club.

A homeless man who sleeps nearby was interviewed by Atlanta Now News. He said the puncture wounds in Freddie's chest must mean it was a satanic ritual gone wrong. He'd seen Pastor Leach from a local church entering through the back door on several different occasions. What other explanation could there have been for the preacher to come out disheveled? He must have been performing an exorcism.

"This is not the direction I'd go in," says Cynthia Barnett, my public defender. I've been convicted of Freddie's murder, and the sentencing is in two weeks. She tells me to write a letter to the judge throwing myself at the mercy of the court. It could be the difference between a life sentence and the death penalty. She strongly suggests that the letter should show remorse, pull at heartstrings, and explain why I had to murder my father.

"I'm just telling it like it is."

She shakes her head and places a clean sheet of paper and pen in front of me. She looks at the gray walls and dirty table.

"It's not like this place gives me inspiration to write," I say.

"Well, try to start over," she says. "Stop making it sound like it's a story you heard about on the nightly news. This is about your life and possible death. Please, do something to help yourself."

"Why? What's done is done. There's no need to open up a can of worms." I push the paper away from me and cross my arms.

"The can has already been blown wide open, my dear. You need to finally tell your side of the story, since you were so reluctant to defend yourself during the trial. When that psychologist said you weren't in touch with your feelings, the jury perceived you as a heartless person. I'll come back tomorrow. Make an effort this time." She calls for the guard.

The door slams shut and for the first time, I realize I'm not leaving prison until I'm dead.

I think about everyone who will be affected when my letter is read in open court. Each of us has secrets. We've lived our lives like compressed balls of yarn, twisted and knotted together, unable to separate ourselves from each other. Once I let my secret go, all the others will unravel. We will all be brought forth to be judged.

THE PSYCHOLOGIST WAS right. I've learned to separate my life into different slots. I think he called it "compartmentalizing." To be honest, I don't really remember my entire childhood. I see images of events, but they are like fuzzy snapshots floating through the wind. They are devoid of time and place.

"Did you ever write down your feelings in journals?" the psychologist asked in the first of our two sessions. Normally, he meets with the defendants once. But he couldn't read me the first time and asked to see me again.

"I barely finished high school. Why would I write down things about my boring life?" I was lying. I still feared Freddie and the people I wrote about in those journals. It wasn't all about my feelings or what the bastard did to us. I wrote down the names of people who came to the club, what they did, and what they enjoyed. I was so scared Freddie would find the notebooks that I hid them in the ceiling tiles of the women's restroom.

Even if I wanted them, the club was on lockdown. Who would be able to cross the crime scene tape? But I told Cynthia about the journals and Cynthia contacted my mother about the best way to retrieve the journals. Ginny came through for once and was very cooperative. I dump the box of journals on the table and the stale stench overtakes us.

Since my mother's name was Ginny, she thought it'd be cute to continue the tradition. It doesn't surprise me that she named us Brandi, Rita, Sherry, Remy, and Bailey. The only job she ever had was serving drinks in dive bars. We weren't boys, so Freddie didn't care what we were called, as long as we didn't show up late for work.

Because of our names, the kids in school called us the Boozy Bitches. The assistant principal tried to make us feel better by telling us the teasing would pass. The truth was our father ran a strip club and our mother was a drunken bartender.

Brandi is our oldest sister. She is Ginny's daughter but not Freddie's. I don't think anyone ever asked who her father is, and it doesn't seem like Ginny will ever volunteer the information. When Ginny's parents found out she was pregnant at fifteen, they threw her out of the house. Ginny and Brandi were on their own until they met Freddie. He claims he saved both of them and they owe their lives to him.

Freddie loved Brandi more than he loved Ginny. Always has. When I was a young girl, I thought Brandi was as beautiful as any movie star. Her fiery red hair and piercing blue eyes made her stand out. Five inches taller than the rest of us, she looked like an Amazon princess. She'd been on the coveted Saturday night shift ever since she could walk in stilettos. After dancing, he sent her back with clients to the private rooms. Then he'd take her to his office for his own sick games.

Last year, Brandi escaped Freddie's grubby little paws. During the weekly poker game, Freddie knew he had the winning hand, but he was running out of money. He was certain the man across the table was bluffing. Yogi, a local celebrity who owns a chain of yoga studios, suggested Freddie bet Brandi.

"I got my truck out back," said Freddie.

"That old thing? If you want to fold . . ." Yogi pushed himself away from the table.

"Okay." Freddie tapped his fingers on the table. He couldn't back out now. Yogi was becoming a national celebrity. His book about living a clean lifestyle had debuted on top of the *New York Times* Bestsellers list. He was important, and Freddie was starstruck by him.

"Show us your hand." Yogi smiled.

Freddie flipped over his cards.

Yogi slowly turned his cards over. He wasn't bluffing.

Freddie coughed. "I'm good for the money."

"No, I want her," said Yogi.

Both men looked at Brandi. She kept her head down.

"Well, do you want to come with me?" asked Yogi.

Brandi nodded her head.

There wasn't anything Freddie could do. A bet was a bet. He couldn't look like an ass in front of the high rollers of Atlanta.

"Don't bother packing your shit." Brandi inched her way over to Yogi. He grabbed her hand and led her away. We never heard from her again.

I'm Rita, the second oldest. It's short for Margarita. Before I was born, Freddie was sure he was having a son. The other dancers said he was so excited. He even talked about moving out to the suburbs. Then I arrived.

"Another bitch," he told Ginny. "And it's as ugly as shit.

Hair as dark as yours."

Ginny shouted, "She takes after you." That's the day he broke her nose. It was a good thing she was still in the hospital after delivering me, because he sure as hell wouldn't have driven her there to get her nose fixed.

Freddie pretty much ignored me until he figured out I was good with numbers. I've been handling the bookkeeping at the club since I was twelve years old.

"You're a dog, but one with a brain," he told me. I'm the only one who made it to the tenth grade. I'm also the only one he never tried to touch. I guess being ugly is a blessing.

"You better keep your mouth shut about what happens here," he warned me. "You're the one cooking the books. If I go down, you go down."

Sherry was born a year after me. She was cursed with beauty, so she was another object of Freddie's affection. She started on the pole when she turned fifteen. I always thought she was the bravest out of all of us. She challenged Ginny about her inability to protect us. Freddie smacked both of them around because of Sherry's smart mouth.

Turns out she really was brave. She ran away when she turned sixteen. She took the bouncer's truck halfway across the country and dumped it somewhere around Dallas, Texas. Some say she's been spotted in Las Vegas, using the skills Freddie taught her.

Remy was always the sensitive one, looking for comfort anywhere she could find it. Her teacher called Social Services when Remy was in elementary school. She had been talking about slashing her wrists and burning us all up in the middle of the night. Some woman showed up a month later and questioned our so-called parents. Anyone with half a brain could see the seven of us living in a broken-down trailer behind a strip club wasn't normal. But she left, satisfied with Freddie's spin on things, and never came back to check on us.

"Go ahead and kill yourself if that's what you want,"

Freddie yelled not two minutes after the social worker pulled out of the parking lot. Remy stopped speaking after that.

Some of Freddie's poker buddies had a waif fetish. Remy's dirty blonde hair made her seem even younger than she was. Freddie started bringing her to the games. Afterward, she would disappear into someone's car and crawl out crying. By the eighth grade, she had wasted away to ninety pounds. She was becoming the nothing Freddie told us we were. She killed herself when she was fourteen. Freddie wouldn't pay for the cremation. Some of the dancers and customers chipped in and paid the nine hundred dollars to the funeral home.

My youngest sister, Bailey, was Freddie's last hope of having a son. He stopped touching Ginny for good after the nurse came out of the delivery room and announced it was a girl. As soon as the words left the woman's mouth, Freddie turned and walked out of the hospital.

For years, Brandi, Sherry, Remy, and the other working girls seemed to keep Freddie occupied. Bailey was always like a doorstop to Freddie. He knew she was there, but she served little purpose for him. But six months ago, he started looking side-eyed at her. His eyes lit up as he watched her wavy, golden blonde hair sparkle under the disco lights.

For the first time, Ginny nagged him about keeping his hands off her child.

"I can do whatever I want. If you don't like it, leave." He shoved her into the bar.

"Karma is going to get you," Ginny screamed.

"Look at you. No wonder I have to look everywhere else. You're disgusting." Freddie kissed Bailey on the mouth before he walked away.

"Someone's going to gut you one day," Ginny cried as one of the topless waitresses held her back.

"Shhh . . . he'll hear you," she warned Ginny.

"I don't care. We can't go on like this."

"Where will you go? Freddie is well connected in Atlanta."

You know you'd never get custody of Bailey."

"I will if he's dead."

GINNY SHOULD HAVE been the prime suspect. No one brought up the threats during the trial. Most of the employees had moved on to other illegal activities and couldn't be tracked down. Public defenders don't normally hire private investigators to back up their clients' stories. I didn't push it.

I was the club manager. I had access to Freddie's office. I was the one who locked up that night. As far as the police were concerned, it had to be me.

Many of Atlanta's finest and sometimes even the Sheriff partied at the club. They were given free access to the back room, and in return they pretended not to know about certain activities. The lead detective in the case played cards with Freddie. They wanted the case closed as soon as possible.

MS. BARNETT RETURNS and I hand the single sheet of paper to her.

"Is this it?" she asks, crinkling her nose.

I nod.

"It says the judge should do what he thinks is best. What the hell are you doing?" She shakes her head.

"Please deliver the journals to Ginny for me. Thank you for all you've done for me." I yell for the guard.

The entire town is holding its collective breath waiting to see if I spill its dirty little secrets. I'm sure community leaders, clergy, music executives, and professional athletes are all scrambling to make certain situations disappear. Ginny says I have enough dirt to blackmail any judge, cop, even some members of the jury.

It doesn't matter if I get life or death. All of us girls can finally be at peace. That's the most sacred thing of all.

The Enlightened One

My first job of the day is to tweet out the class schedule at Harmony Yoga Center. The first twenty students who tweet back can have the coveted spots in the front two rows. After that, it's first-come, first-served.

Classes with the popular instructors close within five minutes. The only vacancies are with the new instructors who haven't proved themselves, but those usually close quickly too as students who can't get their preferred class make their second or third choices.

Yogi, the founder of Harmony, decides at the last minute if he wants to teach class. On a normal day, the line is around the building by seven in the morning. Today, several hundred of the more than ten thousand students who belong to the Center stand in the windy darkness, in the slight hope of catching a glimpse of Atlanta's celebrated yogi and lifestyle guru, Damien James.

Everyone knows Yogi is my husband. Very few people have access to him. Someone like me wouldn't usually have a shot in hell to meet him. But when he won me in a poker game from my stepfather, he just led me away.

"Don't bother packing your things. You're my property now, and you'll have to look the part. We'll have to give you a complete makeover."

The first night he brought me back to his mansion, he ordered me to take off all my clothes as soon as I stepped through the door. He didn't want my cheapness to soil his sacred home. As I stood naked in front of him, he told me he'd stop taking care of me if I fucked up. I had learned from my stepfather how to please men. I kept my head down, trying not to irritate Yogi.

Before he took me to the bathtub to scrub me down, he lit a firecracker and put it in my hands. He then wet his fingers and put out the fuse.

"Every time you piss me off, I'll light this. There will be a time when the wick gets too short to put out before it explodes. Then, you'll be done. Understand?"

"Yes," I tell him.

"Bang!" he shouted at me.

My body shook but I was too afraid to cry.

THE RARE CHANCE to be graced by his presence is typically a recruiting session for The Enlightenment Program. The program allows others to spread Yogi's knowledge to assigned areas around the world. The participants don't have a choice where they move. Yogi has a specific roll-out plan to spread his peace and love, and he won't accept back-talk from any objectors.

Membership begins at fifty thousand dollars and is taught by favored graduates of the program. Additional training, such as personal training by Yogi himself, costs five hundred dollars an hour. The waiting list is thousands long. Some say the First Lady has invited him to the White House, but that may have been a rumor Yogi started himself. There are other programs, where he critiques specific poses, but the price depends on who the student is. The richer the person, the more it costs.

My second job at the Center is to update all our social media with positive affirmations from the leader. The members eat it up and retweet them over and over.

My third and most important task of the day is to retrieve Yogi's organic green tea from Books & Brews. I wash the four thermoses that will take him through the day. He orders special dish soap from the Loire Valley in France—no coloring, no scents, non-toxic, biodegradable. He doesn't risk anything that might affect his health.

The loose-leaf tea package reads: *The tops of the tea leaves are picked by monks on a remote Chinese mountaintop. The monks must train for ten years before they can touch the plant. Mishandling the tea can bruise and damage the tea.*

Yogi is hypersensitive about the tea and how it is served. He will only drink out of a clear mug, free of dyes. If I spill a single drop, he screams like an animal that has lost its young. This is especially true now that he is sick.

"Don't screw it up," he says every time I pour the tea.

I nod and make sure he's happy.

Only a few of his top advisors know he's not well. He's getting weaker every day. The positive side is that he's mellowing. He's been pleasant, actually nice to me. He hasn't threatened to kill or maim me for a while. Behind closed doors, he's thrown a few plates of food at me, but I suppose anyone who is worried about death would do the same thing.

Yogi started feeling tired a few months ago. First, he said it felt like he needed more sleep. Then he developed muscle fatigue. Four weeks ago, he had muscle failure. While he was getting himself a glass of double filtered water, his legs collapsed under him. At first, he blamed me for not knowing he was thirsty and having the water ready for him. But the fear of paralysis made him forget about punishing me.

The kinesiologists on his payroll, who consult with him about his yoga movements, couldn't find a cause for his sudden illness. He brought in the best doctors from around the country and they, too, couldn't give him any answers. Lyme disease, Epstein Barr, and stress were all discussed. Alternative medical professionals, then spiritual healers, then psychics were marched into his office for explanations. He put a shaman on staff to ward off evil spirits. One of Michael Jackson's former doctors is on call 24/7 for vitamin injections.

He's convinced his competition is trying to poison him. He has guards at the office and at the house. I'm the only one allowed to handle his food, drink, laundry, and bathing needs.

His secretary presents me with special gloves we're all required to wear when in contact with him.

This is why he doesn't teach classes anymore. During the video shoots, the chosen few in his inner circle help him get into his yoga positions. The IT crew pieces together the scenes for his online classes. The classes are no longer a live stream.

He's done extensive online research. He's found a kind of gruel made from the tree bark of a thousand-year-old tree. He's paid an African village chief ten thousand dollars to send samples and if he's healed, Yogi promised another one hundred thousand dollars.

Yogi already has a pharmaceutical company ready to chop down the trees and ship them to a laboratory. This healing meal will become a part of a new health program Yogi plans to exploit.

"The healing process might take a while. I'll need you to run things until I'm one hundred percent." He tries to grab my hand, but his reflexes are slow.

I smile.

"You can speak," he says.

I nod. I learned to stay invisible under my stepfather's roof.

"You're not the white trash I thought you were. I value you and I'm sorry." He tries to make eye contact with me.

I walk to the tray of freshly washed mugs and spoons.

"You're the only one I can count on," he tells me. "Will you stay and take care of me?"

I remember the firecracker that is on his dresser, forever there to remind me of my place. How I am under his thumb. How he controls my every breath. I want to light it, tuck it under his covers, and walk away. But I have learned to be patient. I will wait it out.

"Brandi, you've made me see what's important. I need you to help me be myself again." He moans as he tries to prop himself up on his pillow.

In his weakened state, he wants children. He wants to leave

a legacy behind. I don't think I'm capable of loving another human being.

My back is turned to him. I can't see his face, but his voice is low and desperate. He's not remorseful. He's like every other person who hits rock bottom and claims to have seen the light. I don't want him to return to who he was.

I pour him an extra-large mug of the miracle drink I made especially for him.

A Cockroach Never Sleeps

Mother slaps me across the face. It isn't the first time. It won't be the last.

I have come to the nursing home again, pretending to be the dutiful daughter. The nurse shakes her head as she leaves my mother's room.

"She's out of control," the nurse says. "She's . . ."

Although she doesn't say it aloud, I see her mouth "crazy" as she darts out the door. Crazy is a word that could have described my mother at any point in her life. But now her behavior is intensified. And for the first time she's been diagnosed by health-care professionals.

"Mother, did they feed you?"

"They hate me as much as you do."

"Come on, let's get you into bed. You need to rest."

"I fell on the black ice walking to the grocery store. That's why my head isn't right. You had to be fed again. Always eating. That's why you're fat." She points to my stomach and laughs.

"Yes, Mother," I say.

Five years ago, she started to look at me without a sign of recognition. I thought she was playing a new game with me. For the first time, she forgot she hated me. She didn't remember my name is Liz. I was a stranger she wanted to get to know every time she met me. It was a fresh start each day for her.

I was happy and guilty at once. Was I selfish? I, of course, could not start over every day. I could not forget all she had done.

Growing up, no one could know what was really going on in our family. No one could know about the unhappiness, the shouting and the regrets.

But as the years passed by, she let our dirty little secrets slip. Was it guilt, lapses in her defenses, or remorse? I could never tell. She never apologized, only confessing bits and pieces at a time for no apparent reason.

I FOLD HER clothes and put them in her wardrobe closet. It is small, and I imagine no one could fit inside, although my mother insists she hides in there to get away from the scary little girl. The plywood releases a musty odor which reminds me of my childhood hiding place.

My closet was built above the staircase so it was almost as large as my bedroom. It had two levels and I had to climb up into it. The main area was for hanging clothes and the back area was for storage. When she couldn't look at me anymore, she locked me in there. I would climb underneath all the blankets. For a brief time, the warmth of the heavy comforters almost masked the coldness in my life.

I'd practice telling her to shut up. *Leave me alone. I don't have to take this. I'm going to run away. You're an awful mother. I hate you. Just give me away.* But most of the time, I suffered silently, afraid of what else she'd say or do. I listened for footsteps that would rescue me, but they never came. Eventually, she'd unlock the door and I'd climb out from under the blankets. Life went on, until the next time she decided to hurt me.

"NURSE, CAN YOU wash my hair?"

I realize my mother is speaking to me. I put her into the tub and wash her hair. I dunk her head into the water to rinse out the suds. She pushes my hands away.

"Please don't kill me. I told you we would never go back to the beach, and we didn't."

Her voice rips into a cavern of silence. Her eyes widen. She steps back and crosses her arms in front of her face to place a barrier between us. She knows who I am now.

When I turned seven, we went to the beach to celebrate my birthday. I remember her pulling me into the lake to play. This was an odd occurrence because she never feigned interest in me before. But for some reason, I remember not being able to come out of the water. She seemed to be holding me down for a very long time. Then I saw daylight. I assume she couldn't go through with it.

"Mommy, are you trying to kill me?" I asked.

She said nothing because nothing had happened. She claimed I had floated out of her arms. She panicked and grabbed me, causing me to fall deeper into the water. Of course, this was at great risk to her, because she could not swim herself. I was ungrateful again.

I nod.

SHE WANDERS OUT of the bathroom soaking wet and asks me to put make-up on her. I run to her with a towel and dry off her worn body. She looks down at her stomach, pulls at her stretch marks and screams, "Look what you have done to me."

She always told me she was beautiful before I came. She had been the most beautiful girl in her small town. The other girls envied her straight black hair. The boys were mesmerized by her violet eyes. She started modeling for a prominent fashion designer whose name she does not remember. He promised to introduce her to a famous movie producer and gave her an eight-carat amethyst ring to seal the deal. It was only a matter of time before fame would come. I was her only obstacle.

She ballooned from a size zero to an unbearable size six. Her skin stretched out. Her figure was gone. "You scratched my insides, like a cockroach," she said.

As I START applying her eye shadow she says flatly, "Don't let them revive me. You know you died when you were a baby. It's best not to mess with God's plan."

She said I was a sickly baby and never stopped crying. She tried to comfort me one night, but I stopped breathing. She took me to the closest 24-hour clinic. The doctor on duty said it was too late. He would not work on me without a bribe.

"He took my amethyst ring. The amethyst ring! What a waste of eight carats!" she cries.

I know to stand still when she becomes agitated. She wants to make her point and prove she has been a good mother. It is my job to affirm her statements, so I wait for her to finish.

"If I had known, I would have worn my other ring," she says, pointing at her empty finger.

"We'll get you another one," I say.

I WAIT FOR more, but she asks about Dan. She has never done this before. I married a man so much like my father that she'd shudder every time someone mentioned his name.

I came here today to tell her that I'm pregnant. Dan doesn't want the baby. He has already moved on. A small part of me wants my mother to be supportive.

But she doesn't recognize me again.

"Visiting hours are over," the nurse informs me.

I lean against the door and rub my belly. Tomorrow, I will come back and play our little game again—she, trying to remember and I, trying to forget.

The Escape

I closed out my Christmas fund at North Georgia Savings and Loan. With one hundred and fifty dollars and two duffel bags, I planned to run away with Jim, a boy I met at the local junior college.

While I tried to stay invisible, Jim demanded attention. The professor and the other students rolled their eyes as Jim yelled out wrong answers on purpose. He made me laugh and I secretly wished I could be with him.

Jim winked at me one day and my cheeks burned. "Come on, I'll let you buy me lunch," he said.

Each time we met, he told me about his plans to leave Georgia. He wanted to move to Dallas and start a band. He was going to leave all the dream-squashers behind. He would leave with or without me.

"Wouldn't it be good to start over?" He reached over and stroked my hair.

I closed my eyes and nodded.

"OH GOD, IS this what I sent you to school for?" My mother watched Jim saunter up the driveway. She breathed deeply and shook her head. "Is this the best you could do?"

"He's the lead singer in a band," I said.

"He looks like a thug. Your father is rolling over in his grave. If he wasn't dead already, you'd kill him."

"Please, be nice." My hands shook as I opened the door.

"Hi babe," said Jim. He planted a wet kiss on my lips.

"Hey," he said to my mother.

"Mrs. Nixon," she said flatly, her glare ready to set fire to his muddy boots.

"Alright, Mrs. Dixon," he said.

"Nixon," she corrected him.

"Laura, let's go." He smiled with his mouth slightly open, exposing his wad of gum.

"I'll be right out," I told him.

"He'll never be anyone important." My mother clamped her hand around my arm. "I expected this from you."

I tried to hide my nervous delight. "Don't worry. You won't have to deal with him much longer."

"Good. Don't be late for dinner. And don't bring him back here. It's going to cost a fortune to get this mud out of my white carpet." My mother slammed the front door before I could respond.

I had already placed my bags in the trunk the night before while my mother was studying the Good Word. She attended Bible study every Wednesday night, but never quite learned its message.

"Babe, let me drive. You know I can't sit still doing nothing." Jim rolled his hands down my back and set them on my hips.

I looked back at the house to make sure she wasn't watching.

"Let's stop at the gas station." Jim's hand twitched as he waited for me to hand him the keys.

"I filled up last night," I said.

"I need munchies," he said as he jumped into the driver's seat.

Jim peeled into Gas and Stop's parking lot. He bolted out of the car before I could discuss our spending limit. When I caught up to him, he had already piled his sugary snacks on the counter.

"Oh, did you want something?" he asked when I looked at him.

He didn't wait for a response. He swept up his pile of junk food and ran out. Embarrassed, I smiled at the cashier and handed over a twenty-dollar bill. Only one hundred thirty dollars left.

The air conditioning started shooting out hot air around Anniston, Alabama. Jim seemed oblivious to the temperature change. I stuck my head out the window to muffle Jim's dreams of stardom.

I watched the worn-out farmhouses whip by. Old appliances, rusted bicycles, and bales of hay filled the spaces in between. Soon after we passed the "Welcome to Mississippi" sign, I noticed a pale blue dress flapping alone on a clothesline.

Who's this girl living in the middle of nowhere and is she as stuck as I am? I wondered as Jim rattled on about his plans to rule the world.

"Are you listening to me?" asked Jim, realizing I had not spoken for hours.

I didn't answer. I stuck my head further out the window and looked back. The dress danced for a moment and broke free. It tumbled down the highway as if it was trying to catch up to me.

Bucket List

7 A.M.—I type my first Facebook post of the day like clock-work. Staying on schedule is something prison taught me.

Name three places you want to visit this year. What's on your bucket list? Mine are Hawaii, Greece, and Italy.

I throw up a picture of Positano, Italy with its colorful, cliffside houses.

I'll be having grilled octopus and wine very soon. Who's coming with me?

I check number one off my daily list.

9 A.M.—I post a photo of the Mercedes AMG I copied from the local dealership's website.

What color should I get? Black or silver?

I smile when I receive ninety likes on my post.

One of them responds, *Let us know which one you get. Post pictures please!* Forty-two people like that reply.

I get up to stretch my legs and look out the window. I squint. I'm still not used to the brightness of the sun and have to look away quickly. Being outside was the only thing I missed in the eight years, four months, and twelve days I was locked away. When the judge sentenced me to fifteen years, I was relieved. I didn't ask anyone to speak on my behalf, though my pastor's wife came to both days of my trial. Mrs. Leach also visited me once a month in prison, then recommended I be transferred to Second Chances Halfway House. Reverend Leach was a powerful man once, and his word was golden in Atlanta. His approval secured my early release.

The other women at Second Chances worked hard to con-fess, repent, and move on with their lives, but I didn't do any of those things. For me, my crime could neither be forgotten nor forgiven.

11 A.M.—I post, *What is your why?*

In the span of ten minutes, twenty-three people post their responses. The top three are college debt, mortgage, and kids.

Then someone posts a photo of a cherub-like child, approximately five or six years old. *My son is my why.*

I close my eyes and breathe backward from ten. When Pastor Leach was disgraced and removed from the pulpit, Mrs. Leach donated most of his money to charity. She sent a tidy sum to Second Chances. This allowed the founder to hire therapists, yoga teachers, and even a hypnotist to tend to our recovery. One of the yoga teachers taught us how to breathe properly and calm ourselves down.

Ten.

Nine.

Eight.

My son's face flashes in my head. I throw the drenched tissues in the trash and slide the top desk drawer open. His photo is on top.

David. You'll always be my baby. Mommy is sorry.

The doorbell jars me. I put the photo back in its place and peek out the peephole.

"Ms. Moore. Leticia. It's Officer Ramone. I'm here for our weekly visit."

I only open the door for him and for deliveries. I'm too afraid I will accidentally stick my foot out too far and set off the ankle monitor. I practice my smile, exhale, and open the door.

"Officer Ramone, please come in."

"How's everything going?"

"Great!"

When I was ready to leave Second Chances, Officer Ramone suggested I apply for some work from home jobs since I would be on house arrest for two years. My mother died while I was in prison and I inherited everything. I don't think she ever changed her will from when I was a little girl. She had given up on me years ago, when I got pregnant at sixteen and ran off with my drug dealer. She wouldn't want me to have any of this.

"Is there anything you need?" he asks.

"No, I'm getting everything off Amazon Prime, and Cold Fresh delivers the perishables."

"If you need to see a therapist or anything, I can accompany you. I just need two weeks' notice."

"I'm fine. I got my head shrunk enough at Second Chances, even got hypnotized."

"Oh."

"Some sort of regression therapy. It didn't work."

"Well, let me know."

I nod.

"How's the job?"

"Doing great."

After a few moments of continuous silence, Officer Ramone stands up. "Don't be too proud, Ms. Moore. I'm here to assist you."

"Thanks."

"I'll see you next week."

"Okay."

I wave good-bye and make sure the locks are secure. I'm tempted to run my toes through the grass. If I lean out far enough, I can see my childhood playground. How David would have loved the swings. The few times I took him to the small park near our apartment, he squealed with joy.

"Push me higher," he screamed. I was high enough for the both of us. It took years of therapy to admit that. My son didn't die from any illness that he had. He died from mine.

I had stood silently as the judge had addressed me. "Ms. Moore, you didn't ask anyone for a character reference. No one is here to speak on your behalf."

"No ma'am. I'm guilty. I put my son in harm's way. I let him kill my son."

"Ms. Moore, I do hear remorse in your heart. I hope you

can heal. You're hereby sentenced to fifteen years, but it is commuted to eight."

My public defender smiled. It was much less than we expected. Yes, I was passed out drunk while my boyfriend beat my son to death for spilling a cola on his precious Gucci shoes. It wasn't the first time he hit him. I accepted my boyfriend's apologies and guilt-ridden gifts. I wanted a man more than I wanted my son.

1 P.M.—I post on the dozen or so Facebook travel groups I belong to. I snag a picture of a house from a home renovation website.

Oak or bamboo floors? My partner bought this house after six months in the business. Contact me to find out how he did it.

Sixty-seven emails fly into my inbox in the next three hours.

4 P.M.—Harvey Little, my director, texts me: *Are you coming to the annual convention? How can you be an effective leader if you don't attend the most important meeting of the year?*

I smirk. Seven months ago, I saw a Facebook post that Harvey put up on one of the work-from-home sites. I contacted him and asked how he was relaxing in Cancun in the middle of the week.

I read all the books, watched all the videos, and duplicated everything Harvey did. I signed up and started recruiting on all the social media sites that week. I'm his model student. It was difficult at first, not seeing people face to face, but I figured out Facebook videos and posted once a day.

Inspirational quotes from books, Pinterest, even the Bible flew out of my mouth. I said things I'd never heard and didn't believe in, but I did what Harvey said to do.

I prettied up the quotes I stole from Instagram and Pinterest with borders, backgrounds, and photos.

Dreams and hard work are a powerful combination.
She believed and she did.
Do something today that your future self will thank you for.

I have signed up 1,436 people to date. I learned to steer people away from the hot terms: pyramid schemes, scams, and real businesses. "Direct sales" is the new term for multi-level marketing. It sounds professional. It is an action word. Most of the other women on the sites sell make-up, vitamins, jewelry, and all of the companies are run the same as mine. Sign someone up, get paid. Simple.

I've done plenty of illegal stuff—sold crack, prostitution when the boyfriend of the month needed fast cash, and probably other things my blackouts caused me to forget.

Your downline is starting to wonder if you're real. The texts start flying.

I don't respond. I'm Harvey's little gravy train. I will always be grateful to him for my paycheck, but no man is going to ever tell me shit again.

I booked the penthouse for you. It's on me for all your hard work. Let me know if you can conduct a training session. I hear you're the Italy expert.

There it is. He finally said what he wanted.

I put a new couple under you. Sixty-four more people and you're at your next level. A diamond necklace is your bonus. And another $10,000 a month! Anyway, these folks are my cousins. I don't have time to train them so please do me a favor. I'm flying from city to city every night. I need you.

Here is the second thing he wants. He wants to trot me out and show the prospects the success story. I'd love to see New York City, San Francisco, Los Angeles, and D.C. But if I am going to break my parole, I'll be flying to Europe instead.

I send him a Facebook event page link. *Tonight at 7 P.M.*

I post the same post on all my group pages.

6:45 P.M.—I put on my long, blonde wig. Some of my hair fell out from malnutrition in prison and in truth, from drug abuse and alcoholism. I wouldn't fix myself up anyway. Who would I see? I'm home alone all day. It's easier to slap on a wig and red lipstick and put my fake face out in the world every night at seven.

My cell phone dings. Friday. Payday. The company prides itself on its weekly paychecks, and the company delivers. One debit transfer is for booking trips. A second transfer is for recruiting other members. A third transfer is for director-level bonuses. A final ding is for free travel vouchers for booking a high number of trips I can never take.

6:55 P.M.—I pull up the Second Chances website and click the Donate button. I type in *$10,000* and *In Memory of David Moore. He never got a chance to see the world.* I initiate the PayPal transfer.

7 P.M.—I turn on my camera and start the Facebook event.

"Hello Facebook! Please invite your guests now. While we wait, I'm going to tell you how being with this company brings me so much joy. I earned ten free trips this week just by booking travel for family and friends. Yes, I could use them myself, but what did I do? I donated them to the Make-A-Wish Foundation. Win-Win!

"Inbox me if you want to help people like I do. Do you want to travel for free or for a discount? Do you want to earn time freedom and financial freedom? Fire your boss. Work from anywhere. Do what you want, when you want it."

Harvey has checked in, along with four thousand other people. I rub the desk drawer where I've stored David's memory.

I ask my followers what's on their bucket list? It's usually always about travel, cars, and money. It's never about the important things.

ACKNOWLEDGEMENTS

I am forever grateful to Steve McCondichie and the dedicated team at SFK Press for guiding me through this entire process. You all have been patient and kind to this new writer.

I am thankful for those who read the early drafts: Cynthia Tolbert, Sherry Head, Susan Valeri, and Rebecca Hosking. For always encouraging me to continue even when I doubted myself, I am indebted to Sarah Beth Lardie, Mari Ann Stefanelli, Don Lucerto, Melanie Faith, and Elaine Reed. To my photographer and friend, Charlene Gregory, you're the best.

Many thanks to the editors of the following journals, in which these stories, in different versions, first appeared:

Willow Lit Magazine: "American Dreams"; *Gemini Magazine:* "Donor 2000-799"; and *Hamilton Stone Editions:* "A Cockroach Never Sleeps" (originally titled "Memories").

ABOUT THE AUTHOR

Prize-winning writer Yong Takahashi is a first-generation Korean American. Growing up in Detroit with English as her second language, she worked hard to connect lessons of the New World to rules of the Old World. These struggles helped her develop insight into the human psyche and an eye for appreciating the diverse spectrum of humans around her. Yong lives with her husband in Atlanta, Georgia.

She has won the Chattahoochee Valley Writers National Short Story Contest and the Writer's Digest's Write It Your Way Contest. She was a finalist in The Restless Books Prize for New Immigrant Writing, Southern Fried Karma Novel Contest, Gemini Magazine Short Story Contest, and Georgia Writers Association Flash Fiction Contest. She was awarded Best Pitch at the Atlanta Writers Club Conference. Some of her works appear in *Cactus Heart*, *Crab Fat Magazine*, *Flash Fiction Magazine*, *Gemini Magazine*, *Meat For Tea*, and *Twisted Vines*.

SHARE YOUR THOUGHTS

Want to help make *The Escape to Candyland* a bestselling novel? Consider leaving an honest review of this advance reader copy on Goodreads, on your personal author website or blog, and anywhere else readers go for recommendations. It's our priority at SFK Press to publish books for readers to enjoy, and our authors appreciate and value your feedback.

Our Southern Fried Guarantee

If you wouldn't enthusiastically recommend one of our books with a 4- or 5-star rating to a friend, then the next story is on us. We believe that much in the stories we're telling. Simply email us at pr@sfkmultimedia.com.

Do You Know About Our Bi-Monthly Zine?

Would you like your unpublished prose, poetry, or visual art featured in *The New Southern Fugitives*? A bi-monthly zine that's free to readers and subscribers *and* pays contributors:

$100 for book reviews, essays, short stories
$40 for flash/micro fiction
$40 for poetry
$40 for photography & visual art

Visit **NewSouthernFugitives.com/Submit** for more information.

THE NEW
Southern Fugitives

SFK
PRESS

ALSO BY SFK PRESS

CPSIA information can be obtained
at www.ICGtesting.com
Printed in the USA
FFHW022257221119
56113960-62206FF

9 781970 137873